Then Sings My Soul

Then Sings My Soul

a novel by
Sonny Sammons

Cherokee Publishing Company
Atlanta, Georgia
1999

Library of Congress Cataloging-in-Publication Data

Sammons, Sonny, 1942-
    Then sings my soul : a novel / by Sonny Sammons. -- 1st ed.
      p.   cm.
    ISBN 0-87797-281-8
    I. Title.
    PS3569.A4657T48   1999
    813' .54--dc21
                             99-20711
                                 CIP

Copyright © 1999 by John William Sammons, Jr.

This book is printed on acid-free paper which conforms to the American National Standard Z39.48-1984 *Permanence of Paper for Printed Library Materials.* Paper that conforms to this standard's requirements for pH, alkaline reserve and freedom from groundwood is anticipated to last several hundred years without significant deterioration under normal library use and storage conditions.

This book is a work of fiction. Names, characters, places, and incidents either are products of the author's imagination or are used fictitiously. Any resemblance to actual events or locales or persons, living or dead, is entirely coincidental.

Manufactured in the United States of America
First Edition
ISBN: 0-87797-281-8
03 02 01 00 99   10 9 8 7 6 5 4 3 2 1
Edited by Alexa Selph
Design by Kenneth W. Boyd and Pamela Haury Kohn
Cover Art by D. Payne

Cherokee Publishing Company
P O Box 1730, Marietta, Ga 30061

Prologue

Prologue

HIS NOVEL IS BASED on a true story that happened to my family when I was a child. I filled in blanks I didn't know or my relatives couldn't remember. I also changed some names, not all, in order not to create discontent and liability, neither punitive nor pugilistic. The work is fiction based on truth.

The newspaper was calling it a Death Watch. I was a small child but I remember every second. I remember it as the longest forty-eight hours of my life. I've been keeping this story close to my chest for near fifty years now, and the time has come to share it. My grandfather, Alexander Luther Campbell, was the finest man I've ever known. This is the story of how he found himself locked in a cell on death row a few feet from Georgia's electric chair, waiting. Waiting for midnight. Midnight in Reidsville.

Chapter One

HE LONG FUNERAL PROCESSION drove away from the small Baptist church as slow as the pace of a man afoot, and one not in a particular hurry. The mourners had suffered through a grueling forty-five minutes of fist-pounding hellfire and damnation from the Reverend W. R. Cauley, and each came from the church pulling at a tight collar or restrictive corset. Occasionally the reverend had called on God to pave the way for this less-than-perfect subject lying in the casket, to enter the gates that St. Peter corporaled. Mostly he was preaching to scare the shit out of the ones alive.

I was six years old. I was also the center of attention this particular moment. The year was 1944 and World War II was a thousand days old. My father had died in the Pacific theater twenty-one days earlier, in the Mariana Islands. The rosewood coffin that held center stage in front of Reverend Cauley's pulpit, flag-draped and claiming to contain my father's remains, had been borne by six men to a waiting hearse, which preceded our car in the funeral procession.

When the sermon had ended and the final strains of the last hymn were over, my mother, my two grandfathers, Lucy, our maid, my pretty aunt Beth, and myself rode behind the long Cadillac hearse containing a war hero, a man I had seen rarely and known briefly in my young life. We were fourth in the funeral procession. Our car was one of those old limousines that all funeral homes owned. The two rear seats faced each other awkwardly. No one really wanted to sit face to face in situations like this.

The driver sat alone in the front and a sliding glass window partitioned him from the family. The only thing I remember about him was his large ears and the gray tufts of hair growing out of them like cat's whiskers.

The county sheriff, wearing his dress blues, sat rigidly behind the wheel of his car. He led the procession. The red light on top of his patrol car rotated silently. He was also picking up some votes today. He faced tough opposition in 1944. A highly respected veteran of World War I was running against him, and he figured that every funeral he led down the narrow highway toward Eastside Cemetery would ingratiate him to at least the family of the deceased, and maybe even most of the mourners in attendance.

The second car in the funeral procession was a black four-door sedan owned by the funeral home. It carried six men, some old, some unfit for military service. Pallbearers. They would tote my father from the hearse to the family plot at Eastside and his final resting place. Most of my father's old friends and former school-mates were in the employ of the armed services at the present time, attempting to keep the Land of the Rising Sun and the Third Reich from imposing their wishes on the remainder of the civilized world.

Third in line was the hearse containing the remains of Captain Alexander Luther Campbell Jr. He had died piloting a navy torpedo plane while attempting to destroy the dreams of the Japanese sons of heaven and their divine emperor's quest to conquer the Western world. We were the fourth car, and behind us were Uncle James and Uncle Andrew and their families. They were the only two surviving brothers of my grandfather.

A long line of automobiles carrying family friends and well-wishers followed us the last mile my father would ever ride.

I don't remember feeling particularly grief-stricken that day. For me, I suppose, the mounds of fried chicken and cakes waiting at our house, and being attended by some of the older matrons of the town, seemed more pressing and important than the funeral of a stranger who incidentally had the same first and last name as I. My mother was pale and genuinely saddened. I know she loved my father a great deal. Frequently, on the slow ride, I would glance up from the little rend in the car floor rug that I had chosen as the focal point of my sad stare, and she would be wiping a silent tear from the corner of one eye. The tiny blood vessels in her eyes were red and the flesh around her eyes was swollen, so I knew that the sadness had been long and painful. Lucy sat silently next to my mother, and occasionally even she would dab at her eyes with a soft white handkerchief. My father's sister, Beth, cried silently, as she had since early morning.

My grandpa Alex sat on my right side facing Mother, Beth, and Lucy. My grandfather Pete, who I was also named after, sat on my left. Alex would occasionally dig into his right back pocket, pull a crumpled old handkerchief out, and blow his nose so violently the driver would be startled. Pete sat and twisted, shifting his weight from one hip to the other. I knew that his gout was giving him fits.

When I was four, Alex had decided that he was too young and good-looking to be called Grandpa so he instructed me to call him Alex from that day forward. Mother warned me to be prepared, because when Grandpa Pete next heard about this turn of events he'd make me drop the "grandpa" too. Sure enough, the next Sunday, when he made his weekly telephone call, and I told him that Alex and I had gone fishing the day before, he interrupted me and told me to repeat what I had said. He then told me that if my rebel grandpa let me call him Alex, then, "by God, you'd best call me Pete from now on."

Sister Ruby, the daytime operator at the telephone exchange in town, was listening in on the phone. "Pete Sanders! You and that old fool Alex Campbell are for sure going to ruin that boy for life."

"Get off the telephone, Ruby, and mind your own business," Pete told her.

When I hung up the phone, my mother said, "He wants you to call him Pete." More statement than question.

"Yes ma'am."

"Sister Ruby listening in?"

"Yes ma'am."

"I guess by now she's told everyone in town that my father and Papa Campbell have lost their minds." Wiping her hands on a red and white checked apron, she then picked me up and deposited me on the kitchen table. "You are their only grandchild. Each simply wants you to like him best."

The sheriff's car slowed, if it is possible to slow a car already going fifteen miles per hour, to turn right onto the two-rut road that perfectly halved the sprawling cemetery. The Campbell plot extended one-third the length of the cemetery. The order of the founding fathers of the town started on the right and left of the brick columns that guarded the entrance to the only white cemetery in town. Having your family plot one-third the way meant that you weren't at the apex of the social pyramid in town, but that your family had been here long enough to not be considered outsiders anymore. Alex's ancestors stopped here in 1854 and never left. They weren't at the top, but they weren't at the bottom either.

My name is Alexander Peter Luther Campbell.

Alex was a planter. He had been a farmer until his holdings reached three thousand acres. He then announced that he was now a planter. He was the father of my deceased father.

Pete was my mother's father. His roots were in Maine. His ancestors were among the families that dismantled their homes and businesses after the Revolutionary War. Loading them on ships, they sailed north to Canada and established the village of St. Andrews rather than pledge allegiance to a new flag – ninety buildings and homes had been taken down board by board, and reerected in Canada. Pete's family fished, trapped, logged, and numerous other things before returning to the United States at the onset of the Civil War in order to fight with the Union forces. When my mother was a little girl, Pete lost his left leg from just below the knee and would never tell anyone how it happened. He says that sometimes even now his nonexistent toes itch.

Time and biochemistry had treated both my grandfathers with extraordinary indulgences, sparing them both serious reckoning with the nuisances of middle age. They were both physically and mentally vigorous.

The sheriff stopped his car beyond the grave site and immediately got out with his hat over his heart and a remorseful look on his face. He stood at rigid attention as the six pallbearers exited their car and aligned themselves, three to each side of the rear opened doors of the hearse. A hawk-nosed attendant pulled the casket to the rear of the hearse, and the six men took hold and duck-walked to the frame above an open grave six feet deep.

I don't remember much about the minister's next shouted dialogue, but toward the end of his sermon, I don't know what happened, but my mother started crying, Beth started crying, and Alex started crying, so I started crying too.

"Ashes to ashes, dust to dust," The preacher said at last.

Three rigid men in military uniforms had stood motionless a few feet from the grave. Each man had a rifle. The man with the most chevrons on his full-dress uniform had called them to attention when we drove up to the grave site. He ordered parade rest after we were seated, then at the end of the service he quietly called, "Atten-shun! Right shoulder–Arms! Prepare to Fire–Fire!" The three soldiers each shot seven times toward the silent and hidden stars.

On the way home Alex said, "I just hope he sent a bunch of those slant-eyed bastards to hell before they killed my boy." This time Alex blew his nose so hard that everyone in the car jumped.

Sister Ruby and Miss Grace were the last to leave our house that night. They had tasted every dish on the huge dining table, checking the bottoms of the containers to read the names written on the small strips of tape that identified the dish's owner so it could be returned. Each dish was critically reviewed by the two ladies: Norma Jean's potato salad always had entirely too much paprika. Old lady Lewis's fried chicken was never crispy enough. Cousin Sarah's slaw was far and away too watery. If any dish was fault-free, then naturally the contributor must have stolen the recipe from so and so. Sister Ruby and Miss Grace had critiqued every wake and funeral-day table of every white person who had died in recent memory within the corporate limits of Chickasaw County, and anywhere else in the county if they were offered a ride.

Miss Grace was retired from the local school system. She had taught fifth grade. Nobody knew for sure how old she was because she refused to tell anyone, but Alex said she had been here since Columbus's third voyage. She was an old maid, and to everyone's knowledge had never even had a man call on her. On several occasions I overheard Alex describe something that would be extremely difficult as being "about as hard to do as Miss Grace's you know what." Miss Grace's hidden parts were a benchmark for a lot of Alex's descriptive terms. Something of no value whatsoever was "as useless as Miss Grace's you-know-what." A bell that was put on top of the courthouse that had never been rung was "rung more than Miss Grace's you-know-what." When I was little, I once asked him what a "you-know-what" was. "You're going to have to wait until you experience you-know-what, before I tell you." I was more confused than ever.

Miss Grace had inherited a small white frame cottage, decades ago, and had lived by herself until the year after Sister Ruby's husband, Zack, had died. Then Miss Grace had moved in with her. Miss Grace kept her own house though, just in case she ever decided that having company was more tedious than living alone.

As victims of the Depression, the two women had become trained in frugality, and since that time had kept close watch over their personal finances. They were so stingy that they almost parted ways once when they went shopping at the county seat and had to pay a penny each for two twelve-minute intervals on the parking meter. They went to Rose's department store and Sister Ruby bought a nickel pack of needles. When they got back to the car, she discovered that one of the twenty-five needles had a closed eye. While she was gone back to the store to get a replacement, Miss Grace had to put another penny in the parking meter and Sister Ruby refused to reimburse her. The argument took about half the town in as mediators, and the two women refused to speak to each other until the next funeral wake.

Sister Ruby's husband had been the all-around handyman, do-all, and general flunky of Chickasaw County. If a leaky faucet needed a washer, or the grass needed mowing, or the fruit trees needed pruning, then someone would merely pick up the telephone, wind the little ringer on the right side, and say, "Sister Ruby, can you tell Zack to stop by the house at his convenience?"

Sister Ruby claimed that fresh English peas had killed Zack. Alex said Sister Ruby had talked him to death. The doctor said Zack died of a heart attack. Looking back though, I think Zack simply lost interest in living. Zack was a moocher. Sister Ruby made him turn over every dime he made to her. She paid their bills, bought the groceries, paid the coal delivery man in the winter, and the same man for ice in the summer. She gave Zack ten cents a week for his Brown's Mule plug tobacco. Zack had to mooch. If any of the checkers players that hung out around the blacksmith shop had peppermint sticks, or licorice, chewing tobacco, or Chic-lets, Zack's eagle eye would spy the object and invite himself to a portion.

One day the checkers players decided to substitute a candy-coated laxative for the Chic-lets gum to try to moderate Zack's bumming. After spending most of the day in the one-seater outhouse, Zack blamed the fresh English peas Sister Ruby had fixed for his dinner on his dilemma. Sister Ruby had called the lone policeman in town, shrilly imploring him to "Come stop Zack, he's gone crazy, he's pulling up all our English peas. You know craziness runs in Zack's family. His mama was crazy as a bedbug." The policeman patiently explained to Sister Ruby that even though he felt like Zack was doing the wrong thing, he couldn't tell a man what to do in his own garden.

Zack died three days later. Pete commented that he probably did it to prove a point. He wanted to show Sister Ruby that he could do something without following her instructions.

Just to be absolutely certain that the laxative didn't unwind old Zack's clock, the checkers players asked Alex if he would be kind enough to find out from old Doctor Ellis if a stool softener could kill a man. Alex came back two hours later walking slow and looking at the ground as if he had lost his best friend. Eight anxious town loafers watched his slow progress and sad demeanor. One of them blurted, "Goddammit, they going to put us under the jail for killing Zack."

"Fellows," Alex started, still looking at the ground, "since I'm the only one outside yourselves that knows about the laxative, and I'm the only one besides Doc Ellis that knows the real cause of old Zack's untimely and uncalled-for demise, and since I see no obvious reason to create a big disturbance in our fine town, then I have made a decision to keep this knowledge to myself. I do however wish that Zack's widow's house had a fresh coat of that new all-weather paint on it, and the poor woman could sure use a nice indoor toilet." Alex walked away more slowly and more dejected than any of the town loafers had ever seen him. Nobody played checkers for five days. When they left Sister Ruby's freshly painted house, they all told her that it was the least they could do. One of them remarked that Alex Campbell was one fine man. They all nodded in agreement.

ॐ

The funeral was eight hours into the pages of history, and everyone had left our house. Mother and I were in the west end of Alex's house, the place that he and my father had fixed up as a private apartment for us, after my father announced that Hitler must be stopped, and got government permission to join the RAF in Canada. She had cleaned the makeup from her face, had pulled her long hair back and fixed it with an elastic band. Tiny freckles that never got the benefit of public scrutiny were visible now.

Most everyone in town thought my aunt Beth was the prettiest girl ever born here, and my mother to be the prettiest woman to ever come to Chickasaw, even though she did carry the blemish of being a Yankee. This was forgiven, because of the family she married into, because of her caring and generous ways, and because if Alex ever heard anyone say anything derogatory about his son's wife, they would have the fight of the century on their hands.

A tiny knock, uncharacteristic of either of my grandfathers, turned our attention to the door. When we didn't immediately respond, Pete asked if he might come in. "Clemmy, I know this is probably the worst day of your and little Pete's life, and I just wanted to tell you that I'll be here for the two of you when you need me. I think you need to start making plans to come back home with me when you feel like traveling."

Another uncharacteristic knock.

"Clem, Alex here. If it's not too late, might I speak to you and little Alex?"

"Yes, Papa Campbell."

He came in, nose red, acknowledged Pete's presence, and said, "Clementine, I want you to know that ever since Alexander and you got married I've considered you to be my daughter, and when you gave birth to little Alex here, I started loving you like you was my own. Since the passing of my wife, God rest her soul, you and Beth have been the only fine ladies in my life. Now I'd be much obliged if you and little Alex would consider taking over the main house with Beth and just giving me your little apartment to live in. Of course now, Lucy would keep fixing meals for us like she always did, if that's all right."

Pete coughed loud enough to get everybody's attention. "She won't be needing Lucy where she's going, Alex. She and little Pete have decided to go home with me."

Alex looked at both of us, and a false smile played around his mouth. "Clem, he, you, and my daughter Beth are my family. You're the wife of my late son, you've established a life and friends and a career down here." Alex said something then, that I think was possibly the first time that word had ever crossed his lips. "Please, Clementine, don't you and the boy leave me now."

"Well, I'm not leaving Georgia without them. And I'd advise you not to try and stop us," Grandpa Pete said.

"Listen, Pete, you're welcome to stay here in your daughter's house for as long as you want, but she and little Alex don't want to go back up to that frozen wilderness you call home."

"Let me assure you, Alex, she has no desire or intentions to raise my grandson in the blessed South. I say that because ignorance is bliss and the South is certainly blessed with ignorance."

My mother and I were silent observers in this verbal altercation. Our heads oscillated from one speaker to the next as if we were watching a championship Ping-Pong match. I could tell by the unspoken testimony of the tightening of her arm around me and the tensed muscle in her jaw that she was getting more and more frustrated and agitated by this senseless argument.

"Pete, in the South we talk real slow and deliberate, because we think things out before we open our mouths. Up north, from what I've observed, the folks seem to prefer putting their mouths into overdrive while their brain's in low gear."

"Whoa!"

My mother looked at Alex. "We buried my husband and your son today." She looked at her father. "Today we buried the man you called the closest thing you would ever have to a son." She raised her hands above her head, closing her eyes and making small fists. "I will not tolerate this. I, and my son, wish to be left alone. Neither of you have asked him or me what we want." Her voice almost visibly deteriorated. Her body shook violently. "I don't mean this disrespectfully, because I love you both, but if the two of you can't behave like gentlemen, I'll have to ask that you not come back. Now please show yourselves out. I'll have you both for breakfast at seven tomorrow, but if I hear of the two of arguing anymore you won't be invited again."

Properly subdued, the two adversaries left, looking at the floor, perfectly ashamed. When the door closed behind them, they glared at each other, each thinking that it was the other's fault. They stalked to their respective sleeping quarters, muttering under their breaths, each secretly wishing for the other's speedy demise.

Chapter Two

ALEX DREAMED THAT NIGHT of an army dressed in gray. When they marched through the streets of Washington, then Philadelphia, then on to Boston, Alex slept the sleep of the innocent with a smile on his face. He loved my father very much, but he was a realist, and realists didn't blame themselves, or God, or the Third Reich, or the Sons of the Rising Sun for the fate that befell his loved one.

Pete hated the South, he tossed and turned, sweated into his pillow. He hated the humidity, the heat, the gnats. He dreamed of Alex, caught on a sawmill chain feed, headed for a gang saw. He didn't think that he was winning his battle to take his only child and his only grandchild to his precious northland.

Breakfast was a disaster. Beth, still red-eyed, excused herself and went back to her room before the meal began. Both men were gentlemen. This wasn't an avocation either was comfortable with. My mother tried to carry the conversation and make it light for my benefit, trying to make my father's death a bit more acceptable and matter of fact. Her questions directed to my grandfathers were answered with grunts or nods or shrugs. The day after a funeral is probably the worst day. The realization that the person is not coming back starts to sink in, and the "Why me, Lord?" hits.

"Papa Campbell, aren't you honored that our Luther was the first hometown hero to come home from the war? I never have attended a twenty-one-gun salute funeral. I hear that Luther may receive the Congressional Medal of Honor. Posthumously. My God in heaven, posthumously!" The last with free-flowing tears.

"Clemmy, you want me to get Chilie to drive you and little Alex over to the city for the day? I hear tell that the department stores are having annual sales. Chilie Peterson is a mighty fine driver. Taught him myself. His daddy's worked for me since the early thirties and raised the finest crop of young 'uns a man could ever raise. I considered him a true friend." Alex meant well, I know, but today he was clearly ranting. Today he was trying to camouflage his personal grief. Today was the day after he had buried his oldest child. His son. The man Alex had counted on to take over when he got old and tired and wanted to join the checkers players downtown.

The veins in old Pete's temples stood out. His face was turning a brilliant red, and his scrunched-down chin made his lower face and neck swell and take on the characteristics of an animated bullfrog. "Clem, if you need anyone to drive you anywhere, I will be that person."

My experience with the undiluted malice that existed between the two men had been limited until now. I recognized that neither man would feel any appreciable amount of remorse if the other suddenly stopped breathing. Alex smiled sweetly and glanced at my mother to be sure his gesture was duly noted and appreciated. If anybody was going to risk another of her mild rebukes, he certainly didn't want it to be him.

Her father seemed impervious to the new rules his only daughter had imposed. After all he had raised her, he had even threatened to spank her once when she was five, and she had better just remember who her real family was.

"Father, please remember that you are my guest, and I will not allow any disagreements in front of my son."

"Clem, I just don't think that it's proper for my only grandson to be named after myself and him." He gestured his head in the direction of Alex. "And for you to call him Alex instead of Pete."

Alex forsook his newfound sense of propriety and directed his flashfire temper toward my granddaddy Pete. "By God in heaven you old fool, would you suggest that we change the boy's name?"

"Yes, I would, you old fool."

"Whoa." Heads turned. "You gentlemen are excused. I will ask you to join my son and I when, and only when, the two of you have learned to behave."

She let five days go by. I was allowed to go out with Beth or Lucy and visit with the citizens of the farm and the town. Lucy was in a unique position in this situation. She was not a member of the family, but close enough to contribute to the local gossip and to temporarily sate the small town's unquenchable thirst for what was going on. "Them two old men are going to wind up killing one another." I heard this time after time when I was with Lucy. When I was with Beth the curiosity was more abated, or kept silent. Beth was a strange, quiet girl who mostly kept to herself in her room reading or writing. She preferred to take her meals in private and rarely involved herself in family conversations or involvements. She had been so different from the gregarious nature of her father, brother, and uncles that she intimidated Alex in a way, made him feel more comfortable when she wasn't there. That she was highly intelligent was obvious, but she was strange and had a tendency to make anyone in her presence uncomfortable. She and my mother got along well, maybe because my mother never tried to force a conversation from Beth. I liked her, and the times we were together alone, conversation wasn't forced but easy and natural.

She always called me Amigo, Tiger, Squirt, or Swahili.

"It's hard to believe but your father was the only human I ever felt safe with and could talk to. He loved me and I knew it. Now that he's gone you're going to have to take his place. Comprenda, Amigo?"

"Suits me. As long as I don't have to call you Aunt Beth."

Small towns in the South had a desire, born of curiosity and nurtured by downright nosiness, heat, humidity, and sometimes cruelty, to keep up with everyone's business and everything that was going on. The claim was laid for being genuinely concerned for the people inquired about. The truth was that more times than not they just wanted to be the figurehead to spread firsthand gossip. The further down the chain, the more diluted the gossip got and the first tellers were always the more admired and envied.

Sister Ruby and Miss Grace were the icons of the worshipers of gossip. In the telephone exchange, which was located in the center of town on the second floor of a two-story building, Sister

Ruby ruled. The telephone exchange was the Mecca of gossip and she was its high priestess. She also had double, six-paned windows at her back and behind the switchboard, that she constantly monitored when her switchboard was quiet. Sister Ruby had been known to put the mayor on hold when there was an interesting occurrence or serious altercation out on the main street. She had even witnessed Mae Florence stab another black woman who was purportedly sharing in the manhood of her husband. She had seen Mr. C. V. Jones commit suicide.

Mr. C. V. had been the only policeman in town. His hours were dictated by the mayor to be "twenty-four hours a day if necessary, two hours a day preferably." Alex said that C. V. got involved with some bootleggers and was letting them peddle their moonshine whiskey in town. The state revenue department was en route to arrest him when he decided to join the ranks waiting in line outside the pearly gates. Sister Ruby said that he walked out in the middle of the Y-shaped intersection that faced the corner of the building where the telephone exchange was and screamed, "If you bastards want me, you're going to have to follow me to hell to get me."

Alex said that Mr. C. V. was the meanest man to shit between two shoes in all of Chickasaw.

I know that when I went to town and I saw Mr. C. V. with his big silver badge on a chest that was bent and sulking, and with his dark craggy face that contained a permanent frown, and with his brow that was adorned with the longest eyebrows ever grown by man, I knew I was scared. I was positive that God was going to make me pay for what I thought, but I really wasn't sorry when Mr. C. V. took his own life with the same pistol that he had used to send four citizens of our town to their ultimate destinies.

God forbid, but when I was young, as long as the local law enforcement agency didn't interfere with the people in control, then the people in control didn't really care what happened to the less fortunate. Mr. C. V. ensured that the elite never suffered any inconvenience brought on by the less fortunate. When he died he left a family. I don't really know what happened to them—they simply disappeared a few days after Mr. C. V.'s funeral.

Lucy attended the garden club meetings in the capacity of a server of the tea and scones that the white ladies took midway during the meetings. The women paid little attention to Lucy, who would listen to everything that was said and then repeat the conversations to my mother.

Sister Ruby told the garden club that she heard Mrs. Jones talking to her sister. "Now mind you, I'm not repeating gossip, I just happen to innocently overhear the conversation, but it seemed to me a mite unusual that Mrs. Jones didn't cry at the funeral. She was telling her sister that it was a relief, in a way, to get it over with. She said that she had been expecting it. The suicide and all."

"Death comes in threes," Miss Daisy had added to the conversation, "I wonder who will be next. First there was that Campbell boy who got killed in the war, now Mr. Jones. I do wonder who will be next."

Miss Suzy Mae said, "Does anyone know if those two old goats have killed each other yet? Could be that one of them will make the third one. Clementine and that poor girl Beth sure have a heavy cross to bear."

Pete and Alex were both considerably younger than these women, but to a person they all called the two men "old goats."

The truth was, however, that few of its members would have been offended if either of the "old goats" had pursued a possible courtship.

"Give me a break, Clem. I just want what's best for you and the boy." Pete was presenting his case to his daughter ten days after the funeral. "We all would be so much better, the grief would be easier to accept if you were to go back with me."

"I'm not sure what I should do. I teach school. That, and my son are the only things that help me keep my sanity. They are my painkiller. They are my reason for getting up in the morning. I don't think that I can leave here, Father."

"Clemmy, the man is a barbarian. An arrogant old fool who tries to impose his will on all he surveys. He drinks too much, and he plays poker. I just don't think that his influence is best for my grandson. The daughter is so timid and weird that I'm not sure she's even good for my grandson."

"Father, I know he has his faults. So do we all. He loves me and my son just as you do, and leave Beth out of this. She's just different, more ethereal than the rest of us."

"Well, I'm not leaving without you and the boy."

Two more weeks passed, and a passably civilized truce was maintained between the two men. My mother and Beth had them for breakfast and dinner each day. They understood the rules. Fuss, and you didn't get invited back for two days; curse, and you ate by yourself for four days. My mother led the conversation, always asking questions and expecting a complete and pleasant answer. The two men made a valiant effort, each hoping that he might be the one to make my mother see that his way would be best.

The summer passed slowly for me. I was too young to know or understand the deep undercurrents of feelings that flowed and ebbed twice daily during meals around my mother's table. Two strong men, of body and will, accustomed to having their bidding done, were having to act as if they were grade-school children. I wondered how long it would last. I didn't have long to wait. The boil was coming to a head.

Mr. Stewart, the school principal, called on my mother the second week in August. He was a lecherous old man who always scheduled his personal and business calls to coincide with mealtimes. He called on my mother five minutes before our evening meal. Pete and Alex were already there, tight-jawed as usual. Beth came in, and when she saw Mr. Stewart, she made a flimsy excuse not to join the group. I suppose my mother thought that Mr. Stewart would somehow take the edge off a tense situation and invited him to join us.

"Clementine, I really just stopped by to see what your intentions were about teaching this fall." His eyes were focused in the direction of the kitchen, and I could see his nose flaring, smelling the tantalizing aromas coming from that area. "I really do thank you for the invitation. I suppose we could discuss your plans over the pleasures of a home-cooked dinner if it won't disturb your guests." So it was established that Mr. Stewart would be tonight's mediator of the peace, unbeknownst to him.

Appetites were slaked that night. My grandfathers sat attentively, knowing that this was the day of reckoning for Clementine. She would have to put her plans on record. She would finally be forced to divulge her intentions. The air was almost thick with anticipation. Two men, past midlife, waiting with bated breath. I couldn't for the life of me imagine what was so important about where my mother and I lived. I knew my mother and I were important, but I suspected that proud manhood played a part in this drama.

"Mrs. Campbell, I honestly hate to disturb you. Pass the biscuits please, young man. I, uh, the school board. I do believe these pork chops are the best I've ever eaten. Anyway, they need to know what your intentions are, not that we're hurrying you, about teaching your classes this fall. Mr. Alex, would you please pass me a little more of that delicious macaroni and cheese?"

"Mr. Stewart, I need to talk to my family before I give you an answer." She looked at the three of us as if to ensure that Mr. Stewart realize that all our opinions were of equal value. "We're not much of a family as far as sheer numbers go. Only five of us. I would like to keep us all together." She looked defiantly at my grandfathers to let them know that the ultimate decision was hers to make. She continued, now looking at the two of them. Talking to them but making sure that Mr. Stewart knew that she meant the message for his ears. He didn't care, as the meal had his full and undivided attention.

Mr. Stewart wore the same thing every time he emerged from his home for the past twenty-two years. No one knew how many dark blue suits he owned, or how many white shirts and blue ties. Plain black shoes and white socks completed the sameness of his attire, and how many pairs of each he owned no one knew for sure.

Pete said that the cheap bastard probably owned only one of each. Alex, in order not to totally agree, said that he suspected that Mr. Stewart must own at least two of each. Both agreed that neither would ever know for sure unless the man were to suddenly die and Sister Ruby or Sister Daisy were asked to clean out his clothes closet.

She didn't make them wait long. The next morning at breakfast, after making sure everyone had eaten enough, she said, "Beth, if you and these gentlemen will bear with me until I clear the table, I need to talk to you." This was it. This would determine where she and I would live until I reached the majority and was able to decide on my own address. I really didn't care either way.

"You, Pete, my father, had one child and then lost your wife before I knew her, and then you, Papa Alex, lost your wife when your daughter was small and your son was ten. Now it's happened to me. We must be the smallest family on earth to encompass three generations. I don't want to lose any of you, and I don't want my son to be raised without the benefit of the wisdom of his two grandfathers and aunt."

Both men nodded in full agreement. Beth sat wide-eyed. This was the first time she had heard that things may be different.

She stammered, embarrassed, "I don't know what is going on, but if you and my little boyfriend leave, I'm going with you." She looked away, then stood to go as if she had spoken more than was her just due.

"Don't leave. Please, Beth," my mother said before she addressed the men.

"Papa Alex, you said that you would give me and my son this house?"

"Yes, I did. Indeed I did, and I meant it too. Beth, you don't mind do you, honey?" he answered, wondering where this was going.

"I get an insurance check from the military. What I propose to do is to take that money and renovate the guest house. Father, you can live there, and don't tell me you won't leave Maine—this is the only solution I can imagine that will keep us all together."

Pete's mouth dropped open, and his face flushed. He got up and stomped his good foot on the floor, turned completely around two or three times, then stomped his wooden leg. He wanted to curse or object or do something.

"Father, Papa Alex has a crop planted that has to be harvested. Beth needs us as a family. I have a job teaching. You sold your business in Maine. The only ties you have there are the timber land you own, your home, and the cemetery plot where our family is buried. Please don't say anything until I'm finished. My son and I will go with you each summer for as long as you want, to clean around my mother's grave, or anything else you want to do. You don't need to give me an answer yet, just think about it. Father, your grandson needs you. Without you, he wouldn't have a chance to learn the things you taught me as a child."

Alex had an expression of pure, undiluted pleasure on his face. It quickly changed.

My mother turned and looked at him and charged. "Tomorrow, I want you to go to Colonel Jones's law office and get the papers drawn up deeding this house to my son, with my having the power of attorney until he is twenty-one. When you do that, I want you to move your personal effects to our apartment. Beth will stay with us as long as she wants to, and I hope it's forever. If you and my father agree to the terms and conditions of this agreement that I have written down, then

I will agree to stay here and make a home for us all. Another thing. If we do stay and I hear the two of you arguing again, I'll have you both evicted."

Both men were headstrong and accustomed to having their way. This was a strange turn of events, having a diminutive woman with a large voice barking orders and commanding. Neither could decide whether to remain bewildered or to get mad. Both decided to be extremely cautious before they vented anything.

"I might as well tell you that if both of you don't agree to this, then I have an offer to teach in Charleston and I fully intend to accept it. And you can go with us, Beth."

Discomfort and a slight look of concern furrowed the brows of both the listeners. Both realized she was dead serious.

"I will charge you both eighty dollars per month rent and meals. You will alternate weeks paying Lucy. The power bill and all other expenses will be paid by me. We will eat breakfast and the evening meal here. You will have to be responsible for your noon meal. You are not allowed to spend money on my son without my permission. I have opened a college account at the bank for him. Each time you have an overwhelming desire to spend money on him, then add to that account." She paused and looked from one to the other, accessing the impact of her demands, then beseeched them, "Please, will you just please do it. I love you both, but I'm so scared and I want you both to help me raise my child." She was crying now.

If anyone had asked either of those two brave souls the time of day, they would have burst into tears. Fortunately, no one spoke until they were able to regain their composure. Then Beth stood and walked to my mother and the two women hugged and cried. "Just don't go. I've decided to go to boarding school in North Georgia if I can talk Father into that, and I can, and I don't want to come home if you and Sport aren't here," Beth spoke quietly.

Pete, blinking his eyes rapidly, spoke next, "You ever thought to ask little Pete what he wants?"

"The last rule." She started, as if she had suddenly remembered. "I talked it over with my son, and it's acceptable to him. Starting today I will call him Luke, for his father. I would appreciate your doing the same. Lucy will. Do you mind, Beth?" The other woman shook her head and smiled.

Protests from both men begin to surface. Like bile from the unknown regions of the lower intestines the objections started up the alimentary canal then stopped. This was the litmus test, the final objection quelled or not. This was the one thing my mother was willing to compromise on, but didn't want either man to recognize that compromise was in the offing.

Luke was okay with me. I really never liked "little Alex" or "little Pete" anyway.

Both men were thinking that they could probably tolerate this strange turn of events for a short while if my mother thought that this was the right thing to do. Both eyed each other. Both wondered if possibly another funeral might be the solution to a bad problem.

Alex spoke first. "Clementine, I've agreed to each of your decisions, reluctantly, but nonetheless agreed, and by God, pardon me, I'm going to agree to this one too, but I'm giving fair warning that this is about as far as I'm going."

The next morning, still in a God-awful mood, Alex walked to town to collect the mail. As he passed the loafers playing checker pool under the sugar berry tree he exchanged "mornings" then over his shoulder said, "Widow Ruby's grass is getting mighty high." Two men who weren't engaged in the game promptly stood up and headed toward Sister Ruby's house.

Pete had reluctantly acquiesced to the idea of living here and accepting the terms and conditions laid down by my mother. I could tell that he wondered how he went wrong in raising his daughter. He also walked to town that morning, intent on opening his own mailing box and to introduce himself to the telegraph operator at the Central of Georgia depot. He knew that via the telegraph he could conduct his trading just as easily in Georgia as he could in Maine, but he didn't want his daughter to think that this move was any less than a gross aggravation and downright insult to his parental authority. He passed the checker tree also.

"Y'all got gnats up in Yankee land?" one of the locals sang out to Pete as he walked past.

"Yep—assholes too." Pete answered, not even acknowledging the group. Everyone laughed except the asker.

Pete stepped up the two steps that led into the railroad depot and headed for the service counter that separated a stooped and graying Mr. Dean and his ominous telegraph from the rest of the world. Mr. Dean sold tickets on the passenger train that came through town westbound in the morning and returned eastbound in the afternoon. He checked freight, both inbound and outbound. He had a equally old and stooped black drayman named John Smith who followed his orders implicitly with a constant and standard response of "yessar Mr. Dean, sho-nuff Mr. Dean." Mr. Dean also bought excess eggs from the local citizens and the farm folks. Ten cents a dozen. He would count a basket of eggs by reaching into the basket with both hands and grasping one egg between the first-second, second-third, and third fourth fingers of both hands. Declaring a dozen after two trips into the basket with both hands. Everyone said, including Alex, that they didn't know how Mr. Dean did it but he could somehow get thirteen or fourteen eggs out of a basket each time he reached in twice.

"I'm Pete Sanders, and I need to open an account with you to send and receive telegrams. I trade mostly in commodities, occasionally stocks. You can check my credit with the Maine Telegraph and Telephone Co."

"I know who you are, I'm O. Z. Dean, and I'm sorry to hear about your son-in-law. We closed the depot just to go to Luke junior's funeral." The voice was sing-songy. "John Smith, come fetch Mr. Sanders a cup of coffee. Er, Mr. Sanders, we usually charge five dollars to open a new account, but being you're the father of Miss Clementine, I'm only going to charge you four dollars and ninety cents." He looked up through thick glasses as if expecting accolades of praise for his less larcenous proposal.

Pete reached into his right front pocket, got a dime out, and flipped it in the direction of Mr. Dean. "Open the damned account, Mr. Dean, and don't you ever think about trying to steal $4.90 from me again."

Mr. Dean looked through his thick glasses at John Smith. "Nobody's ever questioned me before about the charges. Give me the cup of coffee, John Smith. No sense in wasting it."

Chapter Three

HE NEXT SEVERAL WEEKS passed rather peacefully. Pete was preoccupied with getting his affairs and accounts transferred to Georgia and in order. Alex was harvesting his crops. Beth left for boarding school in North Georgia. We all took her to the train station and she cried and hugged me and said she would see us at Thanksgiving. School started for me, and the halls were teeming with fresh-scrubbed faces. Some of the boys with new overalls with the paper, back pocket flaps still intact, some of the girls with pigtails and patent leather shoes. Boys and girls, either with new shoes and or with bare feet, lined up each morning outside the two-story school located on the east side of town and waited for the bell to ring. Miss Hellman, the principal, was a stern and God-fearing woman. She lived and abided by certain rules that were Spartan and never to be deviated from. Foremost, she believed that to spare the rod was to spoil the child; secondly, she wouldn't allow any student into the building before the bell rang, unless it was snowing, and South Georgia didn't have the audacity to defy Mrs. Hellman and host any blizzards.

My mother taught fourth grade that year, and at my tender age I couldn't understand how she could be so aloof toward me at school. She treated me exactly as she treated all the other first-graders when I saw her between classes in the hall or the lunchroom. Each night she held me close to her and read or made me read, and starting the next morning at eight o'clock she would treat me like every other kid at the damned school. I hated school.

The second-week rebellion welled inside me, and the results marked my debut into notoriety and into the embarrassing position of leaning across a school desk with my backside exposed to the wrath of Mrs. Hellman and her wooden paddle. Alex had bought me a play carpenter's kit, with my mother's permission, from the dime store. The miniature pliers, wrenches, and hammer were resplendent with their chrome coating. God, I was proud of that tool set. The second Saturday after school started I decided that if I took my tiny hammer and walked to the school and tapped all the windows out that I could reach then they couldn't have school anymore. One flaw in my plan—Mr. Willie, the school janitor, was in the basement cleaning the coal-fired furnace that would send steam racing through the radiators come cold weather. The old bastard told on me. Pete, Alex, and Chilie replaced all the windows and I got three beatings and several "Young man" lectures. My mother cried, but she cried a lot anyway.

I repented, as every good boy should, and the following Saturday I was forgiven and resumed receiving the normal rewards for being the object of two doting grandfathers.

Life swept along easily for me the next several months. I can imagine a lazy little creek flowing through a perfect meadow on a butterfly-punctuated fall day. That mental image could symbolize my life for that time. Things came easy for me. I was the son of a schoolteacher, so I was naturally ahead of the other towheaded children in Mrs. Crit's first grade. She held me as an example of the flowing well of knowledge that she aspired for all her students to be. I was hated by many and admired by none. I also got to play the part of "King of the Bees" in the first grade's contribution to the fall school play. Lucy made me a costume using pipe cleaners stuck through a black beanie for antennae and a black-and-yellow-striped T-shirt with cardboard wings attached. For weeks before the terribly important event I would buzz around our house annoying everyone in sight.

One little girl named Rebecca Taylor ignored the other children's disdain for me and became my confederate and my staunchest friend. She was so diminutive that I, even with my short stature, towered over her by almost an inch. This was something I constantly reminded her of. Soon after her declared allegiance to me, a third party joined our ranks. Becky and I voted on whether to accept him into our select group or not. The vote was one for and one against. I, as supreme ruler who was one inch taller, broke the tie and let Washington Jefferson Jackson into our elite group of outsiders. He turned out to be the hard ball sneaked into the beanbag game.

Becky, Wash, and myself did fun things, or what we considered fun things. Both of my newfound friends came from what should have been good-stock parents, dirt poor, but fine and hardworking people. In both cases the mother was the backbone of the family, and she kept, or tried to keep, hidden from the public eye the bad of the father.

Becky's mother and dad owned the pressing club, the town's only garment-cleaning plant. Dry cleaning was a service necessary for those well-off, and a status symbol for the less fortunate. The Saturday afternoon deliveries of the brown paper sheathed clothing items by Becky's father were welcomed by all.

Wash's father was one of the town drunks. He worked hard at the stock yard, but when Saturday came and the weekly sale was over Fox Jackson would beat a straight line to the shot house operated by Lonnie Jakobs, an old black man who had been a major force in the physical building of all the dwellings and businesses built in the past several decades until he broke both his hips in a fall and had to resort to moonshining for a living.

Wash's mother took in washing and ironing six days a week to help fill the gap left vacant from Fox's habit.

By late October the three of us were a fixture around town. After school each day we would run home and change from our school clothes, then meet in the center of town. We searched for thrown-away soft drink bottles that we could redeem for half a cent, and then we would turn the hard cash into candy or full drink bottles. This was the height of the harvest season and the wagonloads of high-piled cotton going to the gin were numerous. Little white cotton gnats made small living whirlwinds over grassy plots but easily parting when we purposely walked through their congruity. Cotton mote from the three gins in town coated the trees and painted landscapes a dirty white between rains. The sweet smell of a ripening earth preparing for winter filled my mind and sense of smell.

Alex told me one night that the winter would come early this year. He explained that the big geese from Canada were flying the fly-ways to Florida earlier than usual and he had added forty more cotton pickers than he normally did.

"Can me and my friends ride with you to check on the weighing-in some time? Maybe tomorrow afternoon?" I asked.

We walked fast to the stock yards after school to make sure Fox Jackson would let Wash go. Becky's family had a phone and I had asked her the night before. Fox's thin, almost skeletal, frame could be seen leading an emaciated white mare toward the two-wheeled road cart that he used to test the stamina of the horses that were sold each Saturday immediately after the hogs and cattle were sent through the round sale ring.

Mr. Roy Watson owned the filling station directly across the street from the sale barn. Loafing benches were built with wide thick boards between the upright posts that held up the tin topped overhangs on three sides of the small brick building. Mr. Roy was a stout man with wispy white hair that looked ever unkempt and a porcelain-skinned face with fine red webbing on his nose and cheeks.

One of the many loafing farmers sitting on the gathering benches rose and walked toward the stock barn signaling for Fox to wait up. "That horse any good, Fox? I need a pretty gentle plow horse."

Fox looked back to make sure his boss wasn't in the vicinity before answering. "Ain't worth a plugged damn, Mr. William. If you need a keep-it-up, all-day workhorse, bid on the black gelding with a white star."

We reached the spot where Wash's dad stood, and my friend waited patiently until Fox and Mr. William were through talking.

"Can I ride out to Mr. Alex's this evening to help weigh up cotton?"

"You need to chop some stove wood for your ma before you do anything. I expect she has several other chores for you too." A tic in a facial muscle and spittle escaping from the side of his mouth were surefire indications that the itch for the soothing white whiskey needed to be salved in the gut of this skinny little man.

Wordlessly Wash turned and trudged off in the direction from which we had just come. When we caught up with him, Becky asked, "Does this mean you can't go?"

"Naw, I was just checking if he had any money in his pockets. He had two quarters."

I thought I knew what he was alluding to but asked anyway. He answered, "My Pa is a liquor head. Two quarters will buy him four shots of liquor at Lonnie's. He won't remember what he told me by the time he gets home tonight."

Nine mule-drawn wagons lined up one behind the other and waited at the end of the big cotton field for the field boss to call for weighing-up time. The sun was falling toward the western horizon and growing larger and the color of a tangerine. A circle of bull bats darted toward the high, plum-colored cirrus clouds that cloistered the darkening sky then plunged and rushed acrobatically for earth, seeking the high-flying mosquitoes that made their evening meal. The low refrains and chorus of spirituals that took their roots from drum beats of Africa could be heard floating across the late afternoon field.

Each of the individual burlap sheets, piled high with fleecy cotton, would be tied, and its owner would wait patiently, straw hat fanning the gnats away, until the two strong men with the cotton scales got to them. A long skinny white oak pole rested on the shoulders of the two men. The scales were located in the center of the pole, and when the men straddled a cotton sheet, the field boss would call out the name of the person who had picked this particular sheet of cotton in a loud voice then hook the sharp hook of the scales into the knot. The two strong men would hoist the pole into the air and the field boss would move the scale pea until the scale was perfectly horizontal. "Sara Mae Cranford, 280 pounds." He would sing out in a musical voice.

When the first wagon had been piled high and packed down with the feet of small children, me and my two friends climbed up the spokes of the wheel and over the top bodies, landing in the soft bed of cotton. The same small white gnats that were in town flitted up and away from our intrusion and flew to more accommodating and hospitable quarters. Vicariously we jumped, then climbed on the wagon seat and jumped more daringly into the cotton destined for the cotton mills up north. In a short five minutes we were doing flips and back flips from the back rest of the drover's seat.

"Ri-i-i-p." The tearing sound of an age-weakened seam could be heard when Wash took his turn and executed a perfect belly flop on the cotton. He tentatively and hopefully felt his rear end, expecting the worst and getting it. He squirmed his bottom half under the protective cover of the cotton and with a firmly set jaw and a red face he refused to move. Wash was so poor that his mother made his underwear out of the chicken feed sacks that she emptied and boiled to soften. The lone thing that would have pried Wash from the protective cover of the cotton would have been for someone to make fun of him, then fur would fly.

"Take your pants off, under the cotton, and hand them to me." Alex said in a quiet voice. "Do it, son. You can stay where you are and I'll bring them back to you in a minute." Alex's sensitive side had felt the boy's embarrassment and responded accordingly. He sent his driver to town in a cloud of dust, and a short while later Chilie Peterson returned with a brand new pair of Red Camel jeans. He told Wash that he figured it would be quicker to put a new pair on Alex's charge account at White's Mercantile than to run down someone to sew the old ones. He told Alex out of our hearing that the jeans were too rotten to sew. The incident was over a few minutes later. Wash had transferred his buckeye, slingshot, and pocket knife to the new jeans and the three of us had decided to watch the weighing-up for the remainder of the day.

Wash wore his brand new Red Camel jeans to school the next day, and one of the insiders questioned why the new jeans.

"Well, I hate to brag," Wash answered, "but, me and Becky and Luke were drinking our third 'big orange' yesterday. I had gas and blew the bottom out of my jeans." Boy, was he obnoxious. Becky laughed until she almost threw up.

The next afternoon we made the same trek to the stockyards, and when Wash determined that his dad didn't have any shot whiskey money, we walked back to the railroad and put a shiny penny on the railroad track. We waited until the afternoon freight rumbled through then retrieved our flattened and unrecognizable penny.

Pete had established a reasonable facsimile of peace with Mr. Dean. They still eyed each other with a mutual distrust each morning when Pete entered the depot, but business had to be attended to. Pete needed the convenience of the telegraph machine and Mr. Dean wanted to make sure my grandfather from Maine wouldn't get him in trouble with the railroad company. Every morning they sat glaring at each other over a checkerboard as Pete waiting for the incoming telegrams that would inform him whether the cotton market had gone up or pork bellies had gone down.

To pass the time between telegrams the two played a game of checkers.

"That'll be three dollars you owe me," Pete indicated to Mr. Dean as he jumped his last checker. The telegraph machine was tapping away and Pete had won six games in a row.

"Ahem. I believe that you counted wrong, Mr. Pete. I don't think you took into consideration the four dollars I won yesterday."

"Yes sir, Mr. Dean, I did take that into consideration, but I was adding back the two dollars and fifty cents I won the day before."

"I'll concede that amount, Mr. Pete, but you seem to be forgetting that I evened that bet up, when you bet me the price of cotton would go up that day, and it fell three cents."

"Well then, Mr. Dean, would you also concede that we be even." Pete said as he tore the tape from the machine and scanned the message. He placed the wide-brimmed felt hat at an exact angle on his head, bid John Smith a pleasant morning, and told Mr. Dean that he would bring doughnuts the next morning and a pound of Maxwell House.

Mary Louise Jackson had walked across the grassy city park carrying a basket full of clean and neatly folded laundry that belonged to Mr. Dean. She held the basket by the two rope handles as she approached the depot entrance. She wasn't paying any attention and neither was Pete when he came through the door. Pete tried to stop at the last second but his weight was on the wooden leg. The next thing either of them became aware of, Wash's mother was sitting flat on her bottom. Her long shirt didn't come up any higher than her knees but her legs were spread apart and Pete Sanders lay face down, his head between the startled woman's knees. Size 44 undershorts and other garments were scattered over Pete and the ground.

Totally embarrassed, Pete extracted himself as gentlemanly as possible under the circumstances. After apologizing profusely, all the while helping Mary Louise to her feet and picking up the scattered garments, he tried to put things in proper order. "Madam, I don't believe we have been properly introduced. My name is Peter Sanders, Clementine Campbell's father, and at the risk of being classed as rude and impertinent, I don't think I have ever knocked down a more beautiful woman in my life."

Blushing brightly, she thanked him for helping her get the laundry up and refused to take the offered money for the messed-up clothing. He brightened even more when she told him that she was little Wash's mother. She was a proud woman, but he wore down her resistance to take the offered money when he told her that if she didn't take it he would give it to her son. She certainly could use it. With Fox's drinking habit to contend with, sometimes the only money for food came from the washing and ironing she took in.

Pete returned through the depot door to a waiting and silent audience of two after the handsome woman walked back across the grass toward her house. After explaining to Mr. Dean that the lady would be a day late with his laundry, Pete found out in detail everything that the considerably knowledgeable Mr. Dean knew about the woman and her family. Pete told the drayman, "John Smith, get your wagon around. I need for you to drive me over to Lonnie's."

Once there, Pete gave Lonnie a few bills to make up for the profit he would forfeit and left with the assurance that Foxworth Jackson would make a dry run the next several times he came to Lonnie's with a powerful thirst. Pete thought long about the pretty woman he had run into at the depot. He tried to dismiss his thoughts as foolish and juvenile but she played on his mind. He made it a point to be extra nice to Wash from that day and always inquired about the health of his mother.

He got one more unplanned chance to see her. Constant and unseasonable rain had interrupted the cotton harvest for Alex, and as the weather had deteriorated so did Alex's mood. Whoever said Grace at our meals always prayed for clear weather too. When the rain finally stopped, Pete, in a rare gesture, offered to help with the weigh-in each afternoon, and Alex, happy to be working, took him up on his offer.

That afternoon I asked, "Pete, can me and Becky and Wash ride with you every day? Alex's in such a sour mood, he ain't any fun."

"Can't say as I blame him. Do you ever see Mrs. Jackson?"

"Yes sir, Wash said that she was real happy that his daddy had come home sober every night for a week."

We were doing flips into the cotton late that afternoon when Wash needed to make a run to the high cotton. He ran down a row to a natural depression where the stalks were higher and the foliage denser than the rest of the field. I heard him scream then saw him run toward us. "I been bit! Luke he bit me! I'm going to die!" He reached the place where several dozen people stood. Wash's face was as white as the cotton piled high on the burlap sheets. When he ran within reach of Pete he grabbed Wash and pulled up his trouser leg. Two little holes spaced about an inch apart were evident in the rapidly swelling calf of Wash's skinny leg.

"Rattlesnake," yelled Pete. "Get the car started." He picked Wash up and ran for Alex's car yelling over his shoulder for me and Becky. He urged Chilie to new heights of speed, speeds that Chilie had never driven before. He came dangerously close to skidding into the ditch several times as he maneuvered the big black automobile around the curves on the dirt road. When we reached the crossroads and turned right toward town, the road was bigger and better graded, but still dirt, and Chilie floor-boarded the car and held his hand down hard on the horn until the town limits came into view. With horn blaring and tires squealing, we made it to the small white frame building that proclaimed itself to be the office of Doctor James M. Ellis, M.D.

"Pretty big fella that bit you, I'd say," Old Dr. Ellis said as he slit the pantsleg of Wash's new jeans that Alex had bought him. The leg was so swollen by now that the normally loose garment leg was stretched tight. "You'll be okay. I'll give you a little shot to kill the snake's venom, and in a few days you'll be as good as new."

A scared Wash wailed out, "Please don't give me no shot, I'd rather be snake-bit." It was too late. Old Dr. Ellis had popped him in the butt with a needle that looked about as long as a pitchfork tine. Wash screamed louder than when the snake bit him.

Two hours later Wash was the hero of the town. We took him home after Pete went by White's mercantile and bought him another new pair of jeans. His pretty momma cried and cried. That night Fox got rip-roaring drunk and got his pistol and yelled that he was going to go kill every goddamn rattlesnake in the county. The only thing we know that he killed was another wide-mouthed jar of shine whiskey.

Becky's mother and father were having problems. "I hear them yelling at each other almost every night," Becky told me and Wash one afternoon as we walked toward the drug store. Pete had seen us coming from school and stopped us to inquire as to the health of Mrs. Jackson, and he gave each of us a shiny new nickel, which we decided to go trade to Mr. Weldon for a triple-dip ice cream cone.

"That ain't nothing," I countered with a lie to impress and best Becky's news about her parents, "Pete and Alex damn near fist-fight every day."

Not to be outdone, Wash one-upped both of us. "Fox comes in every now and then cussing and raising hell and my momma will tell him not to use pruff__, porfanny__, not to cuss in front of me, and when he don't stop, she lays him out for the night with one of them big-handled walking sticks they give to customers down to the stock barn. What're your folks fighting about, Becky?"

"She's caught him rubbing up to one of the scrub girls several times. He's given her a black eye every time she fusses at him about it. If I see him hit her again I'm going to shoot him in the ass with a shotgun. She told me this morning that if she catches him one more time, that me and her are going to live with her mother in Macon."

Dejected and silent at the prospect of the three of us being separated, we trudged on. The drugstore was located on the corner of a small side street that led to an old building that was now an automobile and tractor repair shop. Prior to the proliferation of the internal combustion engine it had been a buggy and wagon manufacturing company. Beyond this building was a cotton warehouse. The narrow alley between these two buildings led to the old city calaboose. We stood in the drugstore on our tiptoes looking through the glass-fronted display case. Our warm breath fogged the glass front. Six three-gallon paper tubs, containing varying degrees of fullness, each with a different flavor, crowded the case. An ice cream hand scoop, which normally rested in a jar of milk-colored water, was in the hand of the waiting Mr. Weldon. He crossed his arms impatiently after a time and tapped his foot as he looked toward the ceiling. We knew time was running out.

"That's it," he yelled. "You act like I ain't got another blessed thing to do except stand up here and wait until you've made up your minds. I'm going to sell this damned ice cream case next week and make the 'Dell' man take that blamed comic book rack outta here. Children don't need to be reading that garbage anyhow, and I ain't got time to wait until sundown for y'all to make up your minds what kind of ice cream you want."

The weather was cold for November, but even at my young age I had discovered that no matter how cold it was you couldn't lick a triple-dip ice cream cone fast enough to keep it from melting all over your hand and sleeve.

After Mr. and Mrs. Taylor closed the pressing club late the next Saturday afternoon, Bertram Taylor cranked the delivery truck and picked up the buxom scrub girl, and for a year no one saw or heard from either of them.

Chapter Four

T HE FOLLOWING MONTH Cayro Taylor petitioned the state court for a divorce on the grounds of abandonment, and Judge Greer granted her the divorce after the mandated time had elapsed. It didn't seem to bother Becky that her father had left them. Alex came home three weeks after Mr. Taylor abandoned his family, and at supper that night he casually announced that he had bought the pressing club from Mrs. Taylor and had hired her to keep running the place. "Chilie's getting fat. I don't need him an hour a day on the farm so he can make all the deliveries and help with the work in the back. Mrs. Taylor couldn't afford a new delivery truck and that old bandit down at the bank wouldn't loan her the money. I swear they ought to make caskets for bankers shaped like corkscrews so's they could screw the crooks in the ground when they die instead of burying them like descent folks."

R. C. Wiley owned the only bank in town, and according to Alex, he had stolen more property, legally, than any man in Georgia. Georgia laws favored the bankers because they traditionally contributed heavily to reelection campaigns and controlled mortgages of politicians. Alex told me that the father of a friend of his had died several years before. Alex's friend had been successful since then, but at the time of his father's death he was broke. When the mortgage on the deceased Mr. Carlton's farm came due old man Wiley had given Alex's friend and his mother twenty four hours to pay the mortgage or lose the farm. Alex went to see the banker on behalf of the widow and R. E. L. Carlton. When Alex asked Mr. Wiley to give them more than twenty-four hours to pay the note, the older banker looked through his bifocals at his railroad watch and said, "You're wrong Alex, she doesn't have twenty four hours, she now has only eighteen hours."

Chilie drove Alex over to Hog Simpkin's house in the next county and Alex told the gypsy livestock buyer to drive over to his farm and look at his cow herd. War was raging in most of the civilized countries of the world and beef was in demand and brought good prices. Alex sold his cow herd. When old man Wiley tried to convince Alex that he wasn't required by law to take his money for the mortgage, Alex reached across the banker's desk and took his phone, pushing the man back in his swivel chair. "Ruby, get the sheriff on the phone and tell him to come to the bank. Then get C. V's sorry ass down here. I want you to call Judge Greer and apologize for disturbing him, but I need for him to come down to the bank. Tell him I'm trying to pay off a mortgage and this crook at the bank won't accept it." Bad blood existed between the banker and Alex since that day.

Old Hog Simpkin was a sight to see. He was so fat that he couldn't fit behind the steering wheel of his big green truck so he hired a wiry black man named Zebulon Pike to drive him and help load the livestock. He bought all the excess livestock that the farm people wanted to sell then he took the stock directly to the packing house forty miles away. A penny postcard, mailed to his address and stating the amount of hogs or cows to be sold, would result in an old green two-ton truck driving into the card sender's yard in less than a week. He could look at a hog or cow and tell the farmer within two pounds what the animal weighed. I always thought that the grossly overweight man possessed a strong resemblance to a hog.

Chilie liked his new position at the dry-cleaner. Delivery men were looked up to and always welcomed when they drove into the clean-swept yards and gently tapped their horns. Chilie bought an official delivery cap, black, with a shiny patent leather bill, exactly like his friend Robert. Robert drove the Atlantic Ice and Coal Company truck, and delivered block ice in the summer and coal in the winter. Our cook Lucy always scolded Robert not to give her a block of ice from the bottom because the truck had hauled coal not long before. Chilie also bought a black short jacket, black trousers, black shoes, shirt and tie. Chilie was a striking figure. Alex told him not to walk dawn the middle of the road at night. "Dammit, Chilie, I don't want you to get run over. I need for you to drive for me." I often wondered why Alex simply didn't drive for himself. He knew how.

The day we were to get out of school for the Christmas holidays, the school hosted a program reminding us who we were and where we were going. We stood and held our hands over our hearts and repeated the pledge of allegiance. Next we sang the national anthem. Mrs. Hellman's shrill voice commanded the top slot in the volume category, and easily could have won the "out of key" national championship if they held one. Two sixth-graders held the United States and the Georgia flags at rigid attention until the music stopped then snapped to parade rest. When the principal announced that our guest speaker today would be a company commander from a training company at Fort Benning, they pulled the flags to attention again as the captain marched across the stage to the podium. He explained to us what we were doing in the greatest war the world had ever seen, then he explained to the upturned faces what our duty should be as patriotic citizens. Last of all he paid homage to all the valiant soldiers that had given their lives in the effort. I rose from my seat between Wash and Becky and walked under the stern gaze of Mrs. Hellman to where my mother sat. I held her hand and she cried the remainder of the program.

Christmas came and a "no holds barred" gift-giving policy was expected by me. Alex and Pete could spoil the hell out of me. All restrictions my mother had imposed would be lifted, and I could get all the presents their generous hearts wanted to give me. They would be many. Christmas morning I ran down the stairs fully expecting to see the tall tree completely obscured by the mounds of colorfully wrapped things that I had carefully circled and marked in the Sears Roebuck catalog. A small scattering of gifts were wrapped and placed under the tree, barely coming up to the lower branches.

After breakfast, which my mother served to an unusually jovial two men, we all adjourned to the living room and I got to open my gifts. I couldn't understand this. Why hadn't these two old fools take this golden opportunity to buy me all the toys I wanted? Wash rode up shortly before noon on a brand new Western Flyer bicycle. The front wheels wobbled profusely but he had managed to ride the half mile without falling. "Thank you, Mr. Pete, for the bicycle. Fox – er, my papa wanted me to give it back to you but my mama put her foot down, and hard."

I tried to act happy for Wash, but the truth was I was envious. I needed a bike too.

That afternoon me and Wash went to the main part of town. He pushed his Western Flyer and I carried my skates until we reached the concrete sidewalk that was limited to the business section. I skated while he rode the bike then we swapped and I tried to ride while he busted his ass as I had done on the skates. Cayro Taylor got a nice Christmas bonus at the pressing club and Becky got a bike also. I was bitter, but not very much. I didn't have time.

January hit the ground flat out and moving toward February. "Why can't I have a bicycle?" I asked my mother for the, according to her, five-thousandth time.

"You can have a bicycle when and only when I think you're old enough. Both your grandfathers wanted to get you one for Christmas." I forgave my grandfathers. Total gift amnesty granted magnanimously by me. I wore her down by mid-February. On Valentines' day I cut out three big hearts from red construction paper that Mr. Weldon had given me, and when she came home that day from the two-story academy, me and Wash and Becky were waiting on the front porch behind the bright red paper hearts. Alex had meticulously written in large black letters across mine, "Roses are red, Violets are blue, Wash and Becky have bikes, I need one too." The next afternoon she got Chilie to drive us to Critt Hardware, and we brought back a brand new blue and white Western Flyer. On the softer ground of the back yard, Chilie would run beside me holding to the seat until I could wobble from one side of the yard to the other without falling. By that weekend the three of us were racing cars down the main thoroughfare leading to town. I acknowledged that if my mother had witnessed what we were doing I would have been returned to the ranks of walking people again until I was thirty years old.

Fox got killed the next Saturday.

Graham Weatherby owned a twelve-hundred-acre farm one mile south of town. His bachelor uncle had raised him after the Asian flu epidemic of 1917 committed Graham's parents to Eastside Cemetery and their final resting place. The land had been in Graham's family since it was given by a land grant from the King of England when Georgia was a British colony and Graham still had the framed document placed above the massive fireplace in the parlor of the two story plantation home he lived in. Graham's not so secret wish was that the south would rise again and the feudal system, prevalent until 1864, would be reinstated and he could ride his big white stallion through slave quarters again.

As was the norm with white land owners in this era of war time prosperity none of them worked other than instructing their field boss or foremen what had to be done that day. By 7:30 each morning the loafing benches around town were full of farmers and planters telling each other what work they were doing that day. Miss Ruby said on more than one occasion that "the only people in this county who work are white women and black men."

Graham had told Fox months before to come find him if any high-spirited stallions showed up at the sale barn. Thinking that a half-pint was the correct stimulus to make sure that Fox did his bidding, Graham had on a weekly basis fed Fox's insatiable thirst for liquor.

Fox sent word to Graham the next Friday that a big Arabian about three years old had come in with a shipment from Capitol stockyards in Montgomery. When Graham rode into town that morning on his aging horse, he stopped by Lonnie's and bought Fox a pint. Fox slipped the bottle in his jacket pocket and made a beeline to the john where he drank half the bottle before capping it and hiding it behind a loose wall plank. He hooked the big horse to the road cart to show Graham what the horse could do, and twenty minutes later the big stallion trotted back past Mr. Watson's service station dragging an upside-down road cart. I got out of school that Wednesday to go with Pete and my mother to Fox's funeral.

The wake had lasted four days, and Pete had sat up each night with the body until all the out-of-town relatives could arrive. Fox wasn't the type of person who accumulated friends, and to tell you the truth, I think everyone recognized that Fox had kind of lost interest in living, so the church wasn't close to full at the service. At the Jackson house after the funeral, Mrs. Jackson came to the small bedroom where Wash slept each night. Me, him, and Becky were back there staying out of the way of the adults who trooped through bringing food and condolences. She asked Wash if he was all right.

"Yes ma'am." She turned to go. He added, "At least he's where liquor won't drive him crazy anymore."

"Mary Louise, what are you and Wash going to do?" Miss Grace asked as she directed the incoming and outgoing people who came to show their respects.

"I don't know, Miss Grace. If I can't get a better job than taking in washing and ironing I guess we'll have to move in with some of my folks in Alabama." In less than an half hour Miss Ruby had told most everybody that "Poor Mary Louise is going to move away."

Miss Grace made the observation for the ten-thousandth time, "You know that death comes in threes. I wonder who we're going to lose next. Be only fair if it was a Methodist this time. The last three out of four were Baptists, other than Fox, and he wasn't a practitioner of the faith."

Thursday morning at breakfast Pete asked Alex if he might have a few minutes to spare that morning. "I need to talk to you about something, and I figured that you would be about as knowledgeable as anyone in town." Before lunch that day the two men drove to Colonel Jones's office and when they emerged an hour later, Pete owned one-half of the pressing club. Three days later, after church, Cayro Taylor stopped by Mary Louise Jackson's house.

Greetings were exchanged and Mrs. Taylor got straight to business. "Mary Louise, Alex Campbell told me this morning that come the first of March he was going to need Chilie more and more and I've got to have some help with the pressing club. The pay won't be but twenty five dollars a week, but you'll get a bonus at Christmas. And Alex said that we could take on your washing and ironing customers and pay you a finders fee of twenty five percent of what you get from them."

"Mrs. Taylor, are you sure about those arrangements? That's more than me and Fox made put together."

That evening after Sunday night service, Miss Grace's second of the three that she forecast passed away, and he was a Methodist.

Alex said at breakfast that it wasn't any surprise to him, he said that old man Linwood, the undertaker at the funeral home, had been eyeing the old gentleman, Mr. Cauley, for months.

Preacher Cauley, as everyone in town called him, was the Methodist minister. His eighty-eight-year-old father had lived with him for the last several years until the night before, when he died. Mr. Cauley was almost an invalid for the last several years. A previous back injury plus the devastating effects of crippling arthritis had bent the man's back from his waist into an almost perfect upside-down L. The few times that Mr. Cauley went outside the house, he would walk with his back horizontal with the ground. Miss Grace said that he had to sleep in a special hospital bed, one that bent in the middle so that the old man's body would be resting on the mattress.

Several of the older men in town usually sat up with the deceased all night, from the time the funeral home delivered it back to the dead person's home, until the day of the funeral. The older men in the Methodist church were all friends of Alex's. The few that usually volunteered to sit up for the wake also had a slight penchant for a nightly toddy. A toddy was a slightly warm drink of water, mixed with a generous amount of 'shine whiskey and toned down with sugar.

The body usually lay in state in the parlor or formal room and the men would wait for all the viewers to pass by the open casket and sign the registry before the jug would be retrieved from its hiding place, which was usually under the floor-length skirting that surrounded the casket gurney.

Mr. Linwood had devised a strap of sorts to straighten the arthritic body of Mr. Cauley and keep him lying straight in the satin-lined casket. The Methodist parsonage had floor-length French-style windows and French doors in the parlor. The gallon jug of whiskey was almost empty at 3 A.M. when the upper strap broke and Mr. Cauley's body sat upright. The next morning after the hardware store opened, they delivered two new windows and the French doors that were in need of being replaced. Mr. Dean said that Alex had the presence of mind to grab the jug of whiskey on the way out of the house when the strap broke, and he reserved his fiercest scowl for anyone that giggled for the next several days. Pete said that old man Cauley probably just wanted a drink too.

March and April filled my life with the wonders of a world that had taken the pall of winter off. Small buds suddenly became yellow flowers, tiny violets poked through last year's leaves, and pale green leaves magically appeared on barren branches. People smiled easily and greeted each other in the streets with a quicker step and a firmer handshake. Even Alex and Pete were cordial at the two meals we shared as a family each day. The cleaning plant was working well and meeting all expenses. As per the two men's agreement, Pete would remain the silent partner and pay the extra money that Mrs. Jackson drew over and above what they would have paid someone to take her place. Both Mrs. Taylor and Mrs. Jackson seemed more radiant and even prettier than they had been when married. Mrs. Jackson was a talented seamstress, and now that she had money left each week after paying her bills, she bought material and patterns from White's Dry Goods and sewed and snipped into the night.

Beth came home when she could.

Everyone seemed happy except my mother. She walked to the cemetery three days each week and took fresh flowers and tidied up the wilted ones. Once a week Alex went with her and visited his son's grave and that of his deceased wife, eight feet away.

I began to notice a marked change in the manner both my grandfathers carried themselves. Alex was fifty-one and Pete was fifty-three. Ancient to me, but in their estimation, not that old. Their demeanor was different somehow, I couldn't put my finger on it, but both men dressed better and kept their hair trimmed and neater. The foxes of the fields and the sparrows of the trees knew the mating call but I was too young to recognize it.

"I'm going to send Chilie down to the pond tomorrow to clean up the cabin and picnic area. I think it's time we had a family outing," Alex announced one morning at breakfast. It was mid-May and the weather was a poet's answer to a perfect spring. His crops were up and growing. Cotton was several inches high and a perfect stand.

"I'll help," Pete added pleasantly. "Dean's company is getting a bit stale of late. A picnic sounds like a splendid idea."

Even my mother got into the spirit of the outing and she and Lucy spent most of Saturday frying chicken and deviling eggs or making crust-free triangle-shaped sandwiches. Pete and Chilie came home at lunch and went back to the pond with reinforcements, and before the day was over, the old site, which had heard young shrieks of laughter many years ago, was ready for young laughter again.

Twenty-nine people showed up. Every invitation had been responded to. Mary Louise had pulled her dark hair back and ringlets trailed down her neck swishing from side to side as she freely laughed. She had sewn a yellow and white polka dot sun dress especially for this day and Pete couldn't keep his eyes off her. Mrs. Taylor wore her auburn hair parted in the middle. Her sensible suit was dark and neat. Before the day was over her jacket was put aside and the top button to her white blouse was unbuttoned. Mr. Dean ate until I thought he would explode and scatter chewed-up food over half an acre.

"Can we go swimming?" I pleaded with my mother. Becky and Wash were at my side to reinforce the request.

"You can take off your shoes and wade in the shallow part. If it's okay with your mothers," she said, indicating my two friends.

We rolled up our trouser legs and in a few minutes we had managed to get wet from head to toe, so we were allowed to wade in our underwear while our clothes dried on pine boughs. Wash had brand new underwear, not homemade from feed bags. Pete took Mrs. Jackson on a boat ride. He paddled strongly and expertly as he had done all his life. We could hear the niceness of her laughter from across the small pond. Mr. Dean dozed at the base of a large pine and Alex read from a book of poetry. Mrs. Taylor and my mother listened to his pleasant bass voice. Some of the guests sat on benches talking. Miss Grace and Miss Ruby played bridge and fussed with two other ladies inside. I thought that if God were a salesman trying to sell a perfect day then today would be his floor sample.

The first late-afternoon whippoorwills were casting their plaintive mating calls. The bullfrogs were tuning up their throaty bass voices for the nightly symphony that would follow. Chilie drove up with three of his friends, and within minutes two guitars, a banjo, and a mandolin were well into blending with the music of frogs and calling birds. Pete built a fire and we roasted marshmallows and wieners. A Yankee had been accepted and he seemed to like the idea.

The last day of school arrived, long anticipated. When it finally did get here and angels weren't blowing clarions, I think we were disappointed. "Let's ride our bikes to the pond and go swimming." Becky suggested when we were dismissed at noon.

She almost drowned that day. When Wash and I pulled her from the water, she wasn't breathing, but I think our pulling her over the ground and then pushing on her chest like we had been shown by the boy scout leader who visited our class actually saved her life. She came up coughing and cursing. Two weeks later she could swim rings around me and Wash, and we kept the near-drowning a secret.

When the Fourth of July arrived and the same group reassembled for a picnic, we surprised them all by diving into the water and swimming far out into the pond. "Becky, come back here this second, you know you can't swim," Mrs. Taylor screamed.

Mrs. Taylor sat on the picnic table, white tennis shoes propped on the bench. She wore medium-length shorts and a halter top, and Alex was having a difficult time keeping his eyes off her. His indiscretion did not go unnoticed by Miss Ruby or Miss Grace.

Chapter Five

ETE SEEMED TO GRADUALLY TAKE to the softer pace and gentler ways of the south. He was a remarkably likable man when he allowed himself to be, and for a goodly period of time lately he acted as if he had abandoned his resourceful disdain for our area of the world.

The less worldly, among whom I counted myself, couldn't understand why Pete had been so agreeable lately. The reason for Pete's change of nature finally surfaced one morning at breakfast. "Ahem, I suggest we get our regular crew together. Alex has to gather his cotton crop and have a fish fry. Pass the biscuits, Luke. And don't forget to invite Wash."

Me, Alex, and Pete had gone fishing the day before, and they had visited the cabin a few times. They didn't fool me. I knew they were having a drink of whiskey. Anyway, Alex decided to put a ladder in the back of the pickup truck to see if he could see any fish and when Pete moved the truck he threw Alex into the pond. Alex was still mad with Pete for throwing him off the ladder, but the prospects of seeing Mrs. Taylor in shorts again clouded any argument he had, and he wholeheartedly agreed. "I think we need to include Dr. and Mrs. Ellis to our list of invitees this time."

My mother absently asked, "Why do we feel the need to invite old Dr. Ellis and his young hussy to our picnic?"

"Clementine! Watch your language in front of my grandson. People might question your raising," Pete chastened, then added, "Why is it, Alex, that you might be taking any sort of interest in that odd couple?"

Alex thought before answering. "Well, the way I see it, Dr. Ellis is the only doctor worth a hoot in hell in the county, and he's got his wagon overloaded trying to keep that woman happy, and I like him as a friend. Least we could do would be to attempt to make his life a little more tolerable."

Dr. Ellis was an avid hunter. He enjoyed the limited free time that he managed to garner away from his practice, in the fields and woods of his many patients. They knew his weakness for hunting, and before the poor man had a chance to bill them, to a man, the land holding patient would extend an invitation to hunt on their property. Dr. Ellis would always lower his charges because of the invitation. He especially liked to turkey hunt. When gobbler season opened in the spring Dr. Ellis would go every morning from opening day until the season was closed.

The Sunday picnics were fast becoming a ritual, wholesomely enjoyed and zealously guarded by all who were invited and, enviably ignored by the uninvited. My mother allowed me to skip church services the times we had the gatherings at the pond. This made me happy. I didn't like Sunday school and I hated the podium-pounding sermons delivered in a near scream by the red-faced minister. Our house always got to the pond first and mother and Lucy covered the tables with red and white checked cloths. Me and Pete and Alex sat on the bench down close to the lake.

"You know, Alex, you ought to build a swimming pool for the children down here, and maybe put a screened room on the cabin. You know, fix the place up real nice. Seems as if everyone enjoys these outings and I can only assume we will continue to have them."

Alex glanced at Pete. "You must think I found the goose that lays golden eggs. These things cost money and I don't see anyone volunteering to help with the cost."

The three of us sat on the bench for a long time staring across the lake and all were thinking totally different thoughts. This was the first week in August, three weeks until the glorious days of doing nothing would end and second grade and Mrs. Hellman would pose a gut-wrenching threat to my laziness. A white and red and black kingfisher sat on a high barren limb of a dead pine across the narrow of the lake. Something attracted the bird's attention, and it dived head-first into the lake, emerging instantly with a small fish.

"I wonder how that damned bird hits the water head-first from that high up without knocking its brain out," Pete said without moving his head. "Reckon how much it would cost to put in a pool and fix the place up?"

Alex cleared his throat. "Those birds are kin to the woodpecker, they all have a layer of liquid surrounding their brain to cushion the impact. I don't know how much it would cost, but if I was to hear any sort of offer to share the cost I would certainly find time to investigate."

We sat there for a time. The two men remained silent.

Pete said, "You seem to know a lot about the natural order of things, Alex. One thing had puzzled me though about your part of the world. We don't have bluebirds up in Maine and I admire their beauty. I've noticed that they have grown lesser in number since I've been coming down here. If you can tell me the answer to that I'll be more than happy to match any contribution you might make toward the children's happiness."

"I'll do my best to explain without rambling too much. You see, the red-cockaded woodpecker pecks holes in the standing dead pine trees and the old utility poles that haven't been treated with creosote, looking for the beetles that infect them. Since the utility companies started treating their poles, the beetles don't inhabit them anymore and the old growth pine has virtually been logged over, the woodpecker is not as plentiful because its food supply has been interrupted. The fate of the bluebird is totally dependent on the woodpecker holes for a nesting place. For every purpose there is a reason, for every reason there is a time. For each thing that happens there is a consequence. A stone thrown in a pond changes things forever for some small thing that lives there. One day there will be no more bluebirds."

At ten past twelve the first guest arrived, and fifteen minutes later twenty-seven people talked loud, laughed, and eyed the food. Miss Grace and Sister Ruby came dressed in the same clothes they had worn to church. Becky and Mrs. Taylor and Wash and Mrs. Jackson came dressed in shorts and sun tops, and I figured that they hadn't been to church at all.

Becky and Wash ran to the pond where I was. I told them, "Alex and Pete might put us in a swimming pool down here if we can figure a way to help get some money. Alex said if somebody helped with the cost he'd put it in."

Four drumsticks and a plate full of deviled eggs and triangleshaped sandwiches must have helped Wash's thinking process. When a reasonably quiet period occurred, he stood up on his bench and shouted. "Mr. Alex, you know that Mr. James down at the cotton gin always gives a dollar a pound for the first bale of cotton that comes in. If you'll take the money from that and spend it on a swimming pool, I'll pick the first bale from your fields next week."

The adults smiled in Wash's direction. Some laughed. Becky stood up beside Wash and shouted as loudly, "Mr. Alex, Luke said that if you had any help that you might build us a pool. I'll help Wash pick the first bale of cotton." I stood up and said, "Me too."

The next morning shortly after sunup, the three of us bravely walked into the head-high rows of cotton. Only a few bolls were open, so our task would be much harder than if the field were fully mature. Chilie had fashioned small gunnysacks into cotton-picking bags for us, and we had them draped across our shoulders as we went from one stalk to the next, picking the cotton that was fully opened. We worked silently, but an occasional "shit" could be heard from my coworkers when the sharp burrs hit tender places.

Two hours after we started, Pete joined us with his cotton sack, and a short while later Chilie drove up and Alex got out and put a bag over his shoulder. That afternoon the count moved up to seven cotton pickers, and the next morning twelve. One day later, Becky, Wash, and I rode the wagon to town. It was piled high with new crop cotton and pulled at a fast clip by a big chestnut horse, just in case someone else was making the same journey with a slower animal.

We got our picture in the paper, along with Mr. Wiley the banker and Mr. James the cotton gin owner. Mr. Wiley had a frown on his face as if to show his disdain for throwing away good money for a bale of cotton that could be bought later on for fifteen cents a pound. He gave the three of us a bank check for $540 and demanded that the three of us come around to his bank and open an account.

Alex pushed off from the pole that helped support the cotton seed bin and walked over and deftly plucked the check from my hand.

"We don't want your piece of paper Wiley. We'll follow you around to your bank and get the cash money, if you don't mind."

The banker's face fell, and a look of undisguised malice settled in place of the usual frown, but he turned and marched toward his bank and the four of us followed.

Pete matched the money that we got for the cotton. Alex took out what he would have gotten for the cotton normally and matched it too. The day Mrs. Hellman paddled Wash for the tenth time, which was the fourth week in September, we swam in our pool. Friends came easy for me after that. Becky decided that when she grew up she was going to marry both me and Wash. That suited both of us.

A killing frost came in late October that year. The winter came quick and was harsh. Leaves that were normally brilliant in color, leaves that when brown would softly petal the ground, leaves that would make perfect catching things for children as they floated toward the earth, were torn by Arctic winds and deposited some place else. Me and Wash had put a wooden stand down at the corner of the state road leading through town and one of the major cross streets that led to the business section. The business section being on the west side of the state road and the oldest residential section lying to the east.

Alex owned the lot. We were selling boiled peanuts and freezing. Becky's mother had made her stay home for the last several days. She said that she needed Becky to help clean the house thoroughly. They were going to have a big Thanksgiving dinner this year and invite all the people who came to our picnics. She told Becky that she might have an announcement to make at that party.

We saw Alex's car coming up the main road. Alex was driving for a change and Chilie was sitting on the passenger side. Down the secondary street that came from the residential section, Mr. Dean, the freight agent, was driving in our direction.

Wash said in a loud voice, "Here comes Mr. Dean toward the stop sign, and here comes your grandpa down the main road. Luke, Mr. Dean ain't never stopped at a stop sign in his life."

It was Saturday morning and a crowd wasn't hard to assemble. The two cars had collided, just as me and Wash suspected they would. After Mr. C. V. killed himself, the city council hired a man named John Justice to be the city constable, and he was duly called to write up the report and assess blame so the damages to the vehicles could be paid for by the driver of fault.

The chief said in an exaggerated show of self-importance, "Can anybody give me an accurate assessment of exactly what happened?"

"It's my fault," said Mr. Dean, the train depot manager.

"No, it's not, O. Z. It's my fault and Chilie can verify that."

"Alex," replied Mr. Dean, "I take the blame. It was my fault. I ran the stop sign."

Chief Justice waited in silence, his accident report book held limply by his side. He felt the need to show his authority but stopped and waited to see which of these two gentlemen would make his report easier.

"Yes sir, you did run the stop sign, but it was still my fault and I take the blame."

"How in the name of hell can it be your fault when I was the one who ran the stop sign?" reasoned Mr. Dean.

"O. Z., I saw you coming, and Chilie, who should have been driving instead of me, saw you coming. Chilie told me it was you coming up the road. Chilie knew you weren't going to stop at that stop sign, and I knew you weren't going to stop at that damned stop sign, so it's my fault."

❧

Reuben Squire got off the big prancing stallion smoothly. He walked toward our peanut stand with the same air of arrogance with which he approached everything he did. He was a big, handsome man. He seemed always sure of himself, and wherever he went, people in the vicinity stopped what they were doing and watched. He wore a black leather jacket cut like a suit coat. Thick black hair stuck out from under a narrow-brimmed Stetson hat, and a white silk scarf kept the chilly air away from his neck. Most of the women in town, both single and married, secretly wished that their shoes were under Reuben's bed. No one in town felt indifferent toward

Reuben Squire. The men either hated him or admired him, but nobody ignored him. Even though Alex didn't like Reuben, he had partially won Alex's respect several years before, when he threw old man Wiley out of the bank window and broke the man's collarbone. Alex thought it was hilarious, but my mother thought it was barbaric. Reuben had a mean streak in him that denied his old mama's gentle upbringing. He liked to hit things. He looked for a fight or trouble the way a good fox hound looks for the spoor of the hunt. He had been married once for a brief time, but rumor was that his wife left him because of his temper.

Reuben had gotten shot in the ankle eleven weeks after the Japanese bombed Pearl Harbor. He had driven to Savannah and enlisted in the army the minute he heard the news of the bombing, and eleven weeks later, he was shot storming a beach on some nameless Pacific atoll. He, like my father, came home a hero, but he came home alive.

"Morning, Mr. Squire," chimed Wash.

"Morning, boys. Give me two bags of peanuts."

"That will be ten cents, Mr. Reuben," I told him.

He handed me a dollar. "Keep the change, Luke. You and Wash tell your pretty mothers to save me a dance at the Christmas charity ball."

He turned and walked back toward his jittery horse. Wash and I felt giddy that he had known who we were, had known our names, and had complimented our mothers so highly. Wash said, "When I grow up I'm going to be just like Reuben, except bigger, and stronger, and more handsome, and richer, and I'm going to be a heap younger."

The horse Reuben was riding skittered away before the man could mount and Reuben took his big belt off and beat the horse with the buckle end until blood dripped. Wash decided he didn't want to be like Reuben anymore.

❧

Before lunch we walked to Becky's house to see if she needed any help cleaning her house. She was mad. "I've told her a hundred times I was going to be a bank robber when I grow up. I hate sweeping and washing and cleaning. You two turkey turds can forget about me marrying you. I ain't cleaning any house for any man. The house I live in ain't even going to have a kitchen."

Wash said, "Call your mama and ask her if we help you finish can you go with us." I thought Wash had lost his mind. He had never, to my knowledge, offered to help anyone with work without there being something in it for him.

When Sister Ruby connected Becky with the dry cleaners, Becky asked her mother and the three of us worked furiously for thirty minutes, then satisfied that the job was ample, we walked to town to spend the money me and Wash had made that morning selling peanuts. We walked to Mr. Idus's white frame store across the road from the cotton gin. We bought a giant dill pickle from a wooden barrel and a penny wheel each. A wagonload of cotton, pulled by two mules and driven by an old black man passed. We waved and Wash asked if we could ride the remaining few yards to the gin. Cotton stuck to the dill pickles but we ate them anyway, frowning constantly. The penny wheels reminded me of a bright sun with rays going in every direction. We ate round and round the brown cookie until only the remaining sun part was left.

We lay on top of the piled-up cotton in the warming sun until it was the driver's turn to pull his load under the suction pipe that would mysteriously suck the contents out of the wagon and into the even more mysterious machines that would separate the seed from the cotton. Forty-five minutes later the piled-up load of cotton would be neatly wrapped in burlap and bound tight with metal straps. The old black man drove his now empty wagon to the platform by the gin press and a big, strong man grabbed the bale of cotton with a metal hook with a wooden handle and tilted the five-hundred-pound bale spinning it expertly into the waiting wagon. A slouchy man came out and pulled a much used pocket ledger from his hip pocket. The old driver signed with an "X" then waved at us before commanding, "giddy-up" to his mules. Another wagon was under the suction pipe, divesting its cargo to the mysterious bowels of the gin, as we walked back toward the center of town.

As we passed the stockyard, Wash's gaze went to the spot against the high wooden fence where Fox usually was when he had free time. He avoided looking at me and Becky, but I saw a tiny silvery tear slip from his face and plummet toward the ground. Becky grabbed Wash's hand and the three of us walked on in the direction of the corner store.

The activity around Mr. Roy Watson's filling station was louder and had more participants than usual. An old Model T Ford was parked in front of the lone gas pump in front of the station. Mr. Roy was vigorously pumping the long red handle at the bottom of the tall tank. The glass receptacle that sat on the top of the pump stand was half full of the bright red fuel. Each successive pump that Mr. Roy made brought a new spurt and gurgle of gas into the glass tank. He pumped with a vengeance until the red liquid reach the six-gallon mark. This was all the ration stamps the driver of the car had and cost an even dollar bill.

Mr. Roy was also furious. He didn't normally pump gas, but his "grease monkey," as he referred to the boy who did the menial tasks around the station, was off today attending his granny's funeral. A few men were lined up throwing an elimination game of quarters to the line. The last one in would plunk down a nickel apiece for the Coca-Colas he would have to buy because of his poor aim. Each man, in order of elimination, would slap a quarter down on the back side of the drink box and pull the cap-up bottle out of the cold water. Each man would feel the bottom of the Coke bottle trying by the Braille method to guess which city his bottle had originally come from. When all the men had deposited their quarters and each had retrieved a Coke, they lifted their bottles up where they could be read, and called out, "Atlanta–got you beat, Montgomery–aw shit, mine's ten miles away–can anybody beat Dallas, Texas?" The bottles were passed for verification of where they were made, and the one with the farthest-away bottle picked up all the quarters.

An old pickup truck was parked across the street from the filling station. It had been painted bright green with a coarse-bristled brush, and in several places the paint had peeled and the original black color could be seen bleeding through. An old man wearing faded overalls leaned against the rear fender. Tobacco juice was spattered down the driver's side door and was also evident in the creases that lined the man's face from his mouth to his chin. Faded blue eyes, the same color as the man's overalls, stared at us from under the brim of a sweat-stained straw hat.

When we came abreast of him, he spit a stream of tobacco juice in the direction of the gutter and said, "I got some mighty pretty puppies on the back of my truck."

Without asking permission Wash climbed on the running board and stuck his head over the truck body. Me and Becky went to the other side of the truck and did the same. Seven squirming puppies about two months old were trying to climb out of the bed of the truck. "How much you asking for these dogs?" Wash asked loudly. I looked at the man to get his answer.

"Twenty-five cents for the males, twenty-five cents for the females, twenty-five cents for the runt."

"The runt ought not to be as much as the big dogs. Most folks give away the runts."

"Take your pick, twenty-five cents."

Becky was over in the truck now, and the puppies were doing battle to see which one could lick her in the face first.

"Where's the mama dog?" Wash asked.

"Got gored by my neighbor's bull."

"That means you ain't got no intention of taking these dogs back home with you."

The pale blue eyes glared at Wash, but the man didn't answer.

Wash came around the truck where I was, and ordered, "Give me sixty cents out of our peanut money." Then he went back to where the man stood and, holding his hand with the money palm out, said, "We'll give you sixty cents for three of them. Take it or leave it."

Hesitating only for a few seconds, the man took the money and when it was safely in his pocket, he swore, "Dammed little thieves, y'all's pa ought to beat the shit out of you."

I picked a solid black male, the biggest of the seven. After minutes of indecision, Becky finally closed her eyes and, feeling for each puppy, said, "Eeny, meeny, miney, moe, how much farther can I go." She pulled the puppy her hand had touched last. It was almost black with brown eyebrows and feet. Wash picked the runt of the litter. It was black and perfect brown circles surrounding the dog's eyes gave it the appearance of having brown sunglasses on.

We walked on, holding our new possessions, and the pale eyed man spit in the direction we were going.

Mr. Weldon yelled, "Don't bring them dogs in here. You young 'uns know I don't allow no animals in here. Wind up getting dog hair in the ice cream. One of these days I'm going to sell that ice cream box. One of you stay outside and tend the dogs, and I ain't got all day while you make up your mind which kind of ice cream you want. Let me see your nickels before I start dipping too."

The only way any of us got to keep the puppies when we got home that afternoon was by telling each of our mothers that we didn't know who the pale eyed man was or where he lived. So we couldn't take them back. We all received stern lectures to never again drag an animal home without permission. That night my dog Inky howled until my mother let him in the house. He promptly went to sleep as my mother carried him to my room.

Becky named her dog Sweetie Pie, and Wash named his Spec. Alex told us, "The first time I see one of those flea bags chasing the chickens I'm going to cut its tail off right behind the ears."

"You do and I'll sic my dog on you," Wash told him.

That tickled Alex and he told everybody he saw that day how Wash had threatened him. Alex was a happy man these days. His cotton crop was bumper, and the cribs around his farm were full of corn. The main thing he was happy about was Mrs. Taylor. She was genuinely fond of Alex. Even a blind man could see that, and he doted on every word she spoke and watched every move she made. Sister Ruby and Miss Grace knew that Alex was sweet on Mrs. Taylor, but they kept the observation between the two of them. Normally a spicy bit of gossip like this would be too much for the women to keep to themselves, but the prospects of Alex getting mad with them and not inviting them to any more picnics took the edge off any desire for idle gossip.

Pete liked Mary Louise Jackson openly and didn't give a damn who knew it. This also took the icing off the cake for the two old women. It's not really good gossip if everyone in town already knows, it's quickly relegated to old news or oft-repeated conversation. Mary Louise couldn't accept any sort of embellished attention from Pete or anyone. It wouldn't be proper. The allotted time as a southern widow in mourning had not elapsed and she didn't want to be the object of wagging tongues.

O. Z. Dean told John Smith that those two old fools ought to be shopping for cemetery plots and arthritis medicine instead of chasing those two young women. "John Smith, they remind me of that old hound of yours that chases the noon freight train through town. What the hell is he going to do with it if he ever catches it?"

John Smith replied, "Speak for yourself, Mr. O. Z. I'm a good ten years older than them two is, and I got myself a twenty-one-year-old girlfriend and she's pregnant."

"Yeah, and if your wife heard you say that, you'd be minus the necessary tools it took to get another young'un. Don't you tell Pete what I said though."

Mr. Roy Watson's wife died last week. I rode by the filling station with Alex and Chilie and a black wreath hung from the door. The benches that would normally be full of the idle were vacant now out of respect for Mr. Roy. All the regular loafers that hung out at the filling station were loafing at different locations until the day after the funeral, when it would be open for business again.

Beth came home on Tuesday for the holidays and she spent most of the day Thursday speeding around the county in Alex's car with me and Wash in the back seat. We passed Reuben Squire riding his big horse on a county road and Beth seemed upset. She finally asked, "Who was that man on that horse?"

Wash answered. "Reuben Squire. That's who. And I'm going to be just like him one day except I'm going to fly in a airplane instead of riding a horse. I'm not going to beat anybody up though. 'Specially a horse."

"Is he married? Not that I care one way or the other."

"Nope. I 'spect he could marry about any woman he wanted to, though."

Alex and Chilie were going to the farm the next morning, and I asked to go along. "Sure you can," Alex answered then remembered. "Go make sure it's okay with your mother first."

Beth was up and helping my mother. She radiated in a way that I hadn't seen before. I asked permission to go. Beth answered. A response that was out of character. "Sure you can go. I'll ride with you men if women are allowed."

Alex was delighted that his daughter wanted to go. He had hoped for years that she would emerge from the shell that she lived in. He babbled on, telling Beth the things she had never asked, or shown an interest in. Halfway the distance to the farm she asked out of the blue, "Do you know anything about Mr. Squire, Father?"

"Reuben? You talking about Reuben, sweetheart?"

"I'm not sure I like that tone you're using. You don't like him?"

"Nobody likes him. You either admire his brass or you dislike him. He won't allow anybody to like him. His old daddy was a harsh critic. Never even allowed anyone to smile in his household. Acorns fall close to the tree."

"Then you don't like him, do you, Daddy?"

"I have no feeling either way, Beth. Ask Chilie about him."

"Sir." Chilie jumped at hearing his name and pretended he wasn't listening.

"Tell her about Squire."

Chilie looked uncomfortable. He didn't want to tell anything, but he knew that Alex had asked him for a good reason. "Before I come to work for your daddy, Miss Beth, my folks owned a little farm that joined old man Squire's land. My pa couldn't read or understand nothing he got in the mail. When I was a boy, old man Squire rode up one morning on a big horse. Reuben was about my age, maybe a couple years older. Big boy for his age. He come with the old man. Mr. Squire told my daddy he had been paying property taxes on this land for seven years after he bought it at a tax sale. Told us to get off the land by next week. My pa started to raise his voice and Reuben came riding over and knocked him down with a long riding crop. He got off that horse just a-laughing. We had to move." He paused, remembering.

꙾

Mr. Roy was added to the list of guests that would be at the Taylor house for Thanksgiving. After forty years of sharing Thanksgiving with his wife, the man was desperately lost.

Cayro Taylor radiated good fellowship and charm that day when we arrived, and anyone with a mean spirit that Thanksgiving morning was soon to give up that mood and become one of the good fellows. She flitted from one guest to the next seeing to their comfort and ease and when she called that dinner was ready and asked Alex to help carve the turkey, everyone, including the grieving Mr. Roy, was laughing and joking. She was a splendid cook and Sister Ruby and Miss Grace had to taste each dish twice before they were afforded anything to be critical of. How she managed to cook and serve for so many people was a marvel. After the meal the men went to the front porch and smoked cigars. The big rocking chairs filled up first and me and Becky and Wash were sent inside for enough straight chairs to seat all the men. We sat on the edge of the porch dangling our legs off and listening to the men swap tales. Dr. Ellis kept the floor, doing much of the talking.

Mr. O. Z. went to his recently repaired and newly painted car and brought back a quart of Canadian whiskey, which he offered around, after taking a generous pull himself. Pete stared at the bottle then at Mr. Dean. "O.Z., that looks suspiciously like a bottle of my liquor." He stated matter-of-factly.

"Pete, I am merely saving you from your overpowering lack of will power to control your intake of spirituous libations. Your liver will thank me one day."

When one woman or another would come to the screened door to inquire about the well being of the men, the bottle would be hastily put out of sight. When it made the lip smacking round, and back to Mr. Dean, only a trace was left in the bottle.

By three o'clock most of the guests had gone, and only Dr. Ellis, Alex, Mr. Roy, and me were left on the front porch. Becky was inside helping her mother and Pete had driven Wash and Mrs. Jackson home in Alex's recently repaired and painted car.

"You been doing any hunting, lately, Doc?" asked Alex, trying to keep the conversation alive.

"Yep, since the fall turkey season came in, I've been going up to that hardwood ridge north of town and calling turkey every single morning. Get up at four o'clock every morning so's I can be up there at least an hour before daylight. I'd rather turkey-hunt than anything else God ever gave us the pleasure of doing."

Alex yawned widely and said, "Good God, Man, you must really like to turkey-hunt to get up that early every morning."

"I almost skipped the morning it rained last week. I left home at quarter after four, like I do every morning of turkey season, and about five, ten minutes later it started raining, so I went back to the house to get my rain suit. I slipped in the back door so as not to wake my wife and found a strange man in my bedroom with her. I tell you what, Alex, it upset me so bad I started not to go hunting that morning."

When everyone had gone except me and Alex and my mother, Cayro Taylor nervously asked us to wait. She said she had something to say and she really didn't know how to tell us.

We sat and patiently waited as she paced the floor. Knowing that the time had come, she said at long last, "Bertram has been writing me, asking for my forgiveness, and begging to come home." She looked at Alex, pleading for understanding, and continued, "Becky needs a father. I'm sorry."

Alex rose from his sitting position and said, "We enjoyed the meal, Mrs. Taylor. Come on, Clementine. Good luck to you, Madam." He walked out the door, and I knew that he was broken-hearted. When he dropped us off at our house, he made an excuse about needing to check something at the farm and sped off. He skipped breakfast the next morning. Pete and my mother stared at their plate and said nothing. I excused myself and got Inky and left to look for Wash and Becky.

Chapter Six

ERTRAM TAYLOR CAME BACK TO CHICKASAW the next week, and Judge Greer remarried the Taylors the following day. Becky was not happy, and Alex got Chilie to drive him to New Orleans. I overheard Chilie telling Pete the next week, "Lord God, Mr. Pete, he had me drive him slam to New Orleans. I didn't know this world was as big as it is. When we left here and got to Alabama all you could see in front of you was more land. I thought sure as the world that we'd run out of land somewhere over there. We didn't get three hours sleep the whole three days we was down there. Man alive that man can drink some kind of liquor."

The DAR sponsored a Christmas bazaar and charity ball each year a couple of weeks before Christmas. Half the money they made went to the Red Cross one year and the Salvation Army the next. The other half went to local efforts. Prior to the war, the Red Cross was the sole recipient of the disbursed half, but returning soldiers told such tales of valor performed by the Salvation Army in the heat of battle on the front lines of each theater of conflict, that the women voted to share the money.

The ball was the social event of the season in our small town. Women, who would have normally been militant leaders of the temperance league, kept their peace, and their heads turned, and allowed their spouses to imbibe this one night and not catch hell. Sister Ruby and Miss Grace took up tickets at the door and critiqued each dress and suit that came through the door. The garden club decorated the school gymnasium for the event and an orchestra from Savannah was hired to play big band music.

Alex didn't want to go, but my mother and Beth insisted that he and Pete accompany them or they wouldn't go. He finally relented and got dressed but swore that he wouldn't have a good time. "I have to admit that the two of you look very handsome dressed up. Beth and myself will be the envy of every woman at the ball," my mother told them.

"Little Brown Jug" was playing when the three arrived, and immediately Pete excused himself to look for Mary Louise Jackson. He found her on the dance floor dancing with Reuben Squire and laughing at everything the man said to her. She was a plain woman when she was married to Fox, but now the instant smile, the freckled face, and the womanly figure made her beautiful, breathtakingly to Pete, and a one-night sexual challenge, for Reuben.

Reuben asked Beth to dance while Mary Louise was in the powder room, and Beth refused but she seemed erratic and nervous. Cayro Taylor and her husband didn't show up that night, and Mary Louise danced almost every dance with Reuben Squire. Pete and Alex got drunk as goats, and Beth had to drive the big black car home. Lucy helped get the two drunks to bed and my mother whispered to each that she was sorry their love lives had turned to shambles.

At breakfast the next morning my mother tried to be cheerful, but despondency seemed to be the order of the day. Pete left to go to the train depot. He had decided at breakfast that he needed an automobile and he was going to catch the train to Thomasville and check other dealers' prices before he came back to Chickasaw to haggle with the two car dealers in town.

An hour later Alex burst through the front doors and shouted as loud as he could, "Lucy, where's my pistol. I'm going to kill that son of a bitch." I was playing with Inky, and my mother was at her sewing machine, making something special. Christmas was only five days away.

Chilie came through the door wringing his old felt hat and begging anyone who would listen, "Don't give him no pistol, he's going to kill Mr. Bertram."

My mother, trying to stay calm but not succeeding, yelled at Chilie, "What happened? What's wrong with Alex? Why is he screaming like that?"

Chilie was almost in tears, "Lawd, we went to the pressing club, and Miss Cayro had a busted lip and a black eye. Mr. Alex took one look at her and started screaming, "I'll kill the bastard.""

Lucy hid the pistol and I hid Inky, in case Alex was mad at him too. Becky couldn't come play with me and Wash for several days. When she was allowed to, the first thing she told us was, "I wish he had never come back. I wish he had stayed with that woman he left with." Me and Wash nodded our agreement.

Christmas holidays were fairly uneventful. Dr. Ellis caught Reuben Squire in bed with his wife, and as the naked man tried to jump the high wooden fence surrounding Doc's back yard, he shot Reuben through the cheeks of his ass with a .38-caliber pistol. When Reuben went to Dr. Martin, the other doctor in town, who was also a friend of Dr. Ellis's, the doctor dipped a cotton swab in Merthiolate and pushed it through the holes in Reuben's buttocks. The nurse told Sister Ruby that Reuben peed all over the examination table.

Alex didn't kill Bertram Taylor. Dr. Ellis forgave his oversexed wife. I didn't get doted on by two doting grandfathers. Damn Christmas. Beth was the only one who would even talk to me, and a lot of what she talked about was Reuben Squire.

❧

January hit like a cold door slamming shut. I hated school. Becky was more and more withdrawn, and Pete and Alex weren't fun anymore. The weather warmed midway in the month, and narcissus, daffodil, and silver bells turned the backyard to fields of yellow and white. I picked handfuls of the sweet-smelling clarions of spring, and presented them like trophies of battle to Lucy and my mother. She quoted me Shakespeare, "Ah daffodil, that shows its head before the swallow date, and paint the winds of March with sweetness."

I hated winter—no one was in a good mood. Me and Wash went by Becky's house almost daily. She would come to the door and announce that her daddy wouldn't let her come out today.

Alex had offered to sell his half of the dry-cleaning plant back to Mrs. Taylor, but she insisted that it would be best if he kept it and she worked for him. Bertram hated the fact that Alex and Pete had bought his business. He also hated them. Alex went to see him one day while no one was home but him.

"Bertram, me and Pete would be more than happy to sell you the pressing club. I'll even finance it for you if Wiley won't loan you the money. The only thing I ask is that you don't ever beat your wife up again. There's nothing more despicable than a man that hits a woman." He leaned closer to maximize the effect and whispered. "If you ever do it again I'll make you sorry."

Becky said that Bertram accused Mrs. Taylor of having an affair with Alex and beat her where it wouldn't show.

Valentine's Day me and Wash took a box of candy to Becky's house. We had sold peanuts at our stand every Saturday when the weather was nice and had taken part of the money for the candy and we missed our little friend. She came to the door and said her daddy had instructed her not to go outside or let anybody in until he came home.

"Where he'd go?" asked Wash.

She opened the door wider and I could see the blackness around her eyes. "Becky, who hit you? Man, you need to come with us. Is your daddy beating you up like this?" She slammed the door and told us to go away.

That night at dinner I told what had happened, and Alex got up from the table and called the sheriff. Sheriff Grimes told Alex that he was sorry, but the only law on the Georgia books that dealt with beating your wife dated back to the 1800s and it only forbade a man to beat his wife more than twice a year. He added that he had no jurisdiction over a man punishing his own child. Alex was furious. He screamed into the phone, "Goddammit, Grimes, make up some criminal charge, you've done it before."

Mrs. Taylor and Becky quit coming to church, and each day when school was out Becky would go straight home. Wash was good company, but I missed her being with us. Wash added spice to my life, but Becky added nectar.

Pete bought a fast little eight-cylinder convertible, called a Stutz Bearcat. He tore up and down the country roads scaring hell out of the people and animals he met in the road. Several times a high strung team of horses would run away, with the hapless driver yelling curses at Pete. Neither he nor Alex paid as much attention to me as I deserved. Me and Wash spent more and more time walking to the creek with Chilie and fishing until the sun went behind the witch hazel that lined the bank on the west side of the creek. We could always make it home by dark if we left when the spindly branches of the witch hazel made the red ball look as if it had been cracked into a thousand different pieces.

Chilie always knew when the fish would be biting. He called it "Mother Nature's humming." He said that some folks heard the rhythm and some folks didn't. I asked him what it sounded like and he told me it wasn't a sound, it was a feeling. The colorful prophecy of rainbows spoke silent messages to Chilie that no one except him understood or heard. The croaking of insects and tree barks and the pelting of animals told him things as a crystal ball told the seer. I gave up trying to understand but I believed him when he said that the fish were biting. It really didn't matter to Chilie if they were biting or not. Alex didn't want Chilie to drive him much lately, and the man was simply trying to occupy his time until Alex got back some of the fire and vinegar in his soul that had been missing as of late.

The first day of spring slipped in. It came, and it was as if God had turned a page from the bad of nature to the good. March 19 was gray, damp, and cold, but when the sun broke its bonds with earth the following morning, a brilliant blue sky greeted the world and transformed the whole countryside into something warm and beautiful. Spring has sprung as Wash would say. Even the birds could tell a difference.

Actually, Wash always said, "Spring has sprung, fall has fell, winter is here and it's cold as hell."

The inner tugging to seed and sow, buried in each person's genes since man began depending on the earth to provide him nourishment, sprang forth and created an overwhelming desire to plant something and watch it grow. I was no exception.

At breakfast I told my mother that I felt like I was going to throw up. Since it was Friday anyway, I figured that it wouldn't hurt to skip school. Just to make sure she believed me, I went into the bathroom and stuck my finger down my throat. After several loud attempts to throw up, I succeeded in doing just that, and she seemed completely satisfied. When she had safely left for school Alex said, "What time is Wash going to get here?" I tried to look betrayed and hurt.

Before I could defend myself, the door opened, and Wash burst in. "Why ain't you in school? When I saw your mamma walking by herself I knew dang-bob well you was playing sick. Howdy, Mr. Alex. How're you, Mr. Pete? What're we going to do today, Luke?"

"You boys want to go fishing?" Pete offered.

"No offense, Mr. Pete, but me and Luke have sat on our butts down at the creek with Chilie every evening for a month. I don't think my tailbone can take another day."

"Why hasn't Chilie been working?" Alex looked at me for an answer.

I replied, "He said didn't either of you have nothing for him to do, and Lucy got tired of him hanging around the kitchen."

"No, he didn't," said Wash. "He said both your grandpas had the 'black bottom, broke-hearted, drag ass, mully grubs' and they wouldn't tell him nothing to do."

Alex left to see if he could think of something for Chilie to do, and Pete laughed and said it was the truth. Chilie had them both pegged right.

"How is your mama these days?" Pete asked Wash.

Wash was leaning against the wall, overalls rolled halfway to the calf of his leg, one thin bare foot on top of the other. He pushed away from the wall and told him, "She's fine. She always asks me if you ever say anything about her."

We went outside, and Alex and Chilie were beyond the barn where we planted a vegetable garden each year. Chilie held onto the plow lines and plow handles expertly. Between Alex's gestures, hand signals, and instructions, Chilie would yell "whup" to the mule hitched to the rig he was obviously about to use. We walked over to watch as the neat row of black earth unfolded over his plow into perfectly curled black waves. Each row ending would charge Chilie to yell "gee" or "haw" to the mule to establish which way he wanted the animal to go. Wash retrieved a mason jar from under the barn, and he and I followed the furrow left by Chilie's plow and picked up long and wiggling red worms, just in case we changed our minds about fishing later that day. We rode with Alex to the pressing club, and while he went in, me and Wash laid in the back seat so that Mrs. Jackson wouldn't see us. She told Alex that Cayro had called in sick.

This was the most perfect day God ever created to goof off. Purple martins were making busy around the rows of gourds that were hung on cross arms atop high poles that provided quarters for the mosquito-eating bird's summer accommodations. Every tree in every yard was filled with the sounds of birds of the same gender. Bees frantic in their flight to beat each other to the next blossom, filled any small sound vacancy left unattended by the birds. The whole world seemed to be in a good mood. Warm spring sunshine affected the energy levels of each living thing to different degrees. Most everything got a rushing need to slough off the winter, so they bustled, or hummed, or flew and flitted. I wanted to go lay in tall grass and let the warm sunshine cleanse my body, and opiate my thoughts. I settled for going with Wash to find some pop-gun elder down by the creek.

At lunch, Lucy fixed some corn bread and vegetable soup made from the tall glass jars of vegetables that lined the pantry. Each year, to accompany the spring garden planting ritual, she makes a mad attempt to use up the remaining jars of vegetables, pickles, tomatoes, and everything else she and my mother put up the year before. Perfect timing to her would be to use the last jar the day before fresh vegetables were ready.

Alex leaned back in his chair after eating a second bowl and said to no one in particular, "It's time to make my peace. Chilie said this weather should hold until first of the week. You boys go by Mr. and Mrs. Taylor's this afternoon and invite them and Becky to the pond for a picnic this Sunday. Unless you want to go to Sunday school instead."

The choice was clear. "I'd rather have a picnic," Wash stated.

There were eight pieces of corn bread left over from lunch, so Wash and I put it in a paper bag and detoured by the calaboose on our way to Becky's house. Three men were in jail. "Y'all want some leftover bread?" I asked.

We stuck our arms through the wire fence and three arms stuck out the bars on the windows. The pitches were near perfect, and all eight pieces were eagerly caught by the extended arms. We left among a flurry of "thank yous" and walked on to the Taylors.

I knocked on the door, and in a few minutes Mrs. Taylor cracked it to see who it was. She looked awful. "Alex asked me and Wash to invite y'all to a picnic at the pond this Sunday. I sure hope you can come."

"That's nice, boys. We might be able to come. Mr. Taylor left this morning on the train to see if he could find a job in Albany. He's supposed to stay with his brother a few days."

Charlie Allman was another of the town drunks. The main difference between him and most of the rest, according to Alex, was that he wasn't a closet drunk. He didn't hide his drinking. He wore it on his sleeve and made a general nuisance of himself. He also owned an old Buick, which he drove like a bat out of hell.

Wash and I were walking the railroad tracks after we left Mrs. Taylor's, our arms extended full out to help balance on the steel rails. I knew that if my mother knew that I walked down the railroad, I could get prepared for the switching of my life.

We saw Charlie's Buick turn the corner by our peanut stand almost on two wheels. He fought to regain control of the heavy car then lost it again. He centered a twelve-inch I-beam, planted deep in the ground many years before by the Central of Georgia Railroad, and sticking up a full four feet. The I-beam didn't budge. Me and Wash were no more than ten feet away when the big car neatly wrapped its front end around the beam and Charlie's head came through the windshield then eased back into the car.

Wash excitedly yelled, "We saw him killed. Boy, I'm glad I skipped school today. Hell's bells, Luke, we can't tell anybody we saw old drunk Charlie get killed. My ma would beat my ass for skipping school."

Twenty or so people gathered around. By the time they got through telling about the accident there wouldn't be as much blood in the hospital cooler as they would describe being all over the car. We had edged closer to the dead man, and Wash nudged me and said, "He ain't dead. I think he's just passed out."

Mr. Linwood turned the corner driving the vehicle that we called an ambulance if you were sick and a hearse if you were dead. He screeched to a stop next to the wreck. Red lights blinked on top of the all-purpose vehicle, and the siren wailed then went silent. The grim-faced mortician jumped from the hearse and opened the rear door, extracting a gurney in one smooth motion. Charlie's still body was on the wheeled stretcher, being pushed toward the gaping rear door when he opened one eye and saw Mr. Linwood, the mortician. He said, "Goddammit, Linwood, I want you to know that I ain't dead, before I go back to sleep. In case you're thinking of anything funny, I got witnesses."

Mr. Carlton, the mayor of Chickasaw, was in the crowd of onlookers. He walked over to the stretcher and pulled Charlie's eyelid up. "When you get out of the hospital come down to city hall and tell the clerk to call me. You'd be better off by far if you let Linwood take you on to the funeral home and embalm you, Charlie." The mayor of Chickasaw was a tremendously big man, with no neck, and lots more muscle than brains. His method of dispensing justice in the small town usually included harsh words or physical violence or both. On more than one occasion when the perpetrator of a nonviolent crime came before the mayor's court and couldn't afford a fine, the mayor made the offender lean across his desk and his wide cowhide belt extracted justice from the man's fanny. The method was crude, but repeat offenders were scarce.

Chapter Seven

HE NEXT DAY MAYOR R. E. L. CARLTON wound up in the same hospital room with drunk Charlie. The mayor was a drunk too. A wild man when he had too much liquor, but he was a different kind of drunk. He would go on a tangent, ripping and roaring around Chickasaw County, then when he had beat up everything from jukeboxes that offended him to utility poles that got in his way, he would sober up and stay sober for several weeks. Most everybody in the county knew when he was on one of his binges, and stayed clear of the man. He was the undisputed strongest man in the county, and when he started drinking, any provocation would be validation for him to tear things up. When he was sober, a gentler, more compassionate man couldn't be found, but strong drink brought out the Mr. Hyde in him.

That night was Friday night, the end of God's perfect day to goof off, and I had gotten away with it, no thanks to Lucy. Mayor Carlton got rip-roaring drunk and rode around town looking for things to beat up. He shot out a street light that offended him by shining too bright, then he sent Mr. Carswell, the night policeman, running for the cover of the firetruck when he shot over his head to wake him up. He woke Lonnie up at three o'clock and got more whiskey.

Going east along the railroad tracks near the city limits, the streets on either side of the track followed the natural terrain of the land then suddenly elevated twenty feet above the tracks until the natural hill went back to the same elevation as the tracks. The banks of the roads were clear except for kudzu that was allowed to grow unchecked to keep erosion to a minimum.

When the morning freight train came through town early on Saturday and woke Mayor Carlton, who was sleeping in his car by the depot, he decided that he would blow this hick town and ride a flatcar to Macon. He kept pace with the fast-moving, empty flatcar across the main intersection and down the street. When he came to the high banks, he aimed his Studebaker automobile over the bank of the road. It rose high into the air and couldn't have been more perfectly timed. The only problem that arose was the bulkhead on the front of the flatcar. The mayor's head went through his windshield when he hit the bulkhead and he wound up in the same room with Charlie.

The next day was Sunday. For me and Wash, a day without worship. We went to the pond early with Chilie to clean the dead bats and leaves out of the pool. Chilie mowed the grass, while Wash and I scoured the picnic tables with baking soda and Clorox. At ten o'clock Pete and Alex drove up in separate cars and all of us worked like ants until my mother and Lucy came back with Chilie, who had been sent to fetch them. Green clover, with a low profile, surrounded the cabin, making a lush carpet of the best weave nature had to offer. Tiny violets shyly poked their beauty from under a layer of last year's oak leaves. An army of big orange and black cow ants marched to a silent drummer through the leaves and up the rough bark of a shag hickory. I was as happy as a full pig in the sunshine, as Alex would say.

Mrs. Taylor and Becky arrived at noon. Becky held tightly to her mother's hand. Cayro Taylor wore makeup to try and hide the bruise on her cheek, but no one at the picnic missed the telltale mark. After greetings were exchanged, Dr. Ellis took Cayro for a long walk across the pond dam and back up the side road that circled through the woods until it came back to the cabin. If anyone noticed, they could see him stop occasionally and talk earnestly to the woman.

Becky came around slowly, but by the time her mother and Doc Ellis came back, she was at ease with Wash and me. Alex was a fine actor; he didn't show any of the anger that was scorching his insides. After a fine lunch, when Pete and Mr. O. Z. went to search the trunk of Mr. O. Z.'s car, Alex politely told them, "No thank you. I wouldn't care for a drink this afternoon."

Pete looked curiously at Alex and inquired, "Are you ill-afflicted Alex? I've never known you to turn down a sociable drink before. Come to think of it, I've never known you to turn down an unsociable drink either."

Mr. O. Z. giggled, and Alex looked coolly at the two. He didn't think an answer was necessary.

Dr. Ellis let his young wife take the car home, and he rode with Alex that afternoon when the party broke up.

Alex was quiet at dinner that night and he excused himself early, saying he thought he would go on to bed. Immediately after breakfast the next morning he left without any explanation.

Sister Ruby's switchboard was positioned in the upstairs telephone office so that when she wasn't busy connecting calling parties she could look out the front windows onto the triangle that was the busiest part of town. From her vantage point she could see the train depot and all the commerce, that was a matter of course, which took place around the freight and passenger terminal. She saw Alex hanging around one of the outside benches that were placed on the east end of the train station to take advantage of the morning sun on cold days. She absently wondered what he was doing there as she heard the morning train chugging and whistling from the east.

Sister Ruby's view of the depot was blocked by the smoke-belching engine and five passenger cars until it deposited its incoming passengers and collected the mail, freight, and passengers going west. The train blew the final blast on its whistle and slowly chugged away from the station, leaving wispy traces of steam and the faint smell of burnt oil. When the red caboose exposed the east side of the depot, Sister Ruby's eyes fairly bugged out. There was Alex and another man rolling around on the ground; occasionally one or the other would land a solid blow to the head or body of the other one. They rolled apart and staggered upright and Alex knocked the other man down. Even though both men's faces were bloody and their clothes half torn off Sister Ruby recognized Bertram Taylor.

Picnics or no picnics, this was more than Sister Ruby could bear. No red-blooded woman should ever be expected to keep news like this to herself. Her fingers expertly flew to the switchboard; her eyes never left the scene by the tracks.

Bertram rolled over and jumped to his feet and plowed into Alex. Alex was waiting and hit him again in the face, knocking his again to his knees. From that position, Bertram lunged for Alex's knees and knocked him flat on his rear. Mr. O. Z. and John Smith could be seen peeping around the corner of the depot. Bertram managed to get two good licks to Alex's head, half-closing one of his eyes.

Dr. Ellis had walked up, grinning from ear to ear. He yelled out loud enough for Sister Ruby to hear, "Round ten, gentlemen."

Alex pushed Bertram away and came off the ground mad and fighting wild. He met the man, twenty years his junior, with fists flying. Ten licks to the face and head later, Bertram's knees buckled and he pitched headlong into the dirt. Dr. Ellis said, "You're losing ground, Alex. I've seen the time when you could have beat that man's ass in a quarter the time you took today."

"Patch the bastard up, Doc, and put it on my bill."

"I don't doctor on skunks! Call the veterinarian."

Mr. O. Z. called from the corner of the building. "The morning freight brought Pete a fresh case of Canadian whiskey. I don't 'spect he'll miss one little bottle. You gentlemen come on in. John Smith fetch us three clean glasses."

"You mean fo' glasses don't you, Mr. Dean? I happen to like Mr. Pete's liquor too."

The mayor got out of the hospital that afternoon and called a special meeting of the city council. They passed an ordinance making it illegal to beat your wife within the city limits of Chickasaw. Mayor Carlton called on Bertram the next morning and explained the consequences of breaking that law, if anybody showed up in his court after violating it. He offered Bertram a job at his saw mill and peace reigned in Chickasaw for a while. Pete got mad as hell at O. Z. for stealing another bottle of his liquor, and Sister Ruby said forty dozen times, "I saw the whole thing. Pow-pow." She would swing one arm then the other. "Pow-pow."

Mrs. Taylor smiled more now and Becky could play with me and Wash until an hour before Bertram got home from the sawmill, then she had to run home and clean house. Since Wash said that he wasn't ever going to get married, I told Becky that I would marry her. She said that she wanted two husbands so that she could get one to beat the other one up if he misbehaved.

One week was left before school was out for the summer, and the children in our school were wild as jackrabbits. When Mrs. Hellman left the room that morning, Wash told the class, "I'm going to break the school record. I'm going to get fifty whippings this year." He already had forty-two. I had gotten eight from Mrs. Hellman, and another eight when I got home.

I asked Wash how he stood it, after the forty-eighth beating took place. "Every time I decide to get a beating I wear five pair of under shorts and put several handkerchiefs in my back pockets. Don't even feel it."

The day school was out, we were dismissed before lunch, and Wash and Becky walked with me to our house and ate lunch. Alex came in whistling and in a good mood. "I've brought in three of the oldest mules from the farm for you children to ride this summer, if you want to. You can keep them in the barn by the garden. The only thing I ask is that you feed and water them good every day, and make danged sure they don't get out and in the garden." He hesitated, then added. "Er, this is our little secret and I don't want you to tell your mother."

Too excited to finish lunch, we ran to find Chilie, so he could show us how to put the reins on the mules. I'm sure by late afternoon that day those mules wished they were back on the farm pulling a plow. In an alley, that ran between White's Dry Goods and the cotton buyer's office, the city maintained a long row of hitching rails. We slid off our mules and walked to Mr. Weldon's.

On the right side of the street, about half the distance between Mr. Weldon's drugstore and Mr. Roy's filling station, was the other drugstore in town. A small-framed pharmacist with a completely bald crown and gray-brown tufts sticking up from the sides of his head owned this apothecary. His big bald dome and small facial features reminded everyone of the cartoon character "Pogo," so he was christened "possum" by the townspeople and there wasn't one in fifty who could tell you his real name. This was where the unproductive went on Sunday mornings when Mr. Roy and the blacksmith shop was closed.

Possum stayed in a different stratosphere from the rest of us earthlings a good portion of the time. Ordinarily, by late afternoon, he was as high as a buzzard in August riding the thermals. Alex said he took "goof balls." He said that when Dr. Ellis prescribed painkillers for a suffering patient, Possum would substitute sugar pills and take the drug for himself, getting around the narcotics agents who checked the pharmacist's records.

Me, Becky, and Wash were on the opposite side of the street when Possum's front doors burst open and a young black man ran toward Mr. Roy's. Possum charged out into the street waving a pistol and yelling "Stop, thief!" He fired the pistol in the general direction of the running man and struck the full gasoline bulb on top of Mr. Roy's gas tank. The gasoline splattered over Graham Weatherby's roadster, and the thick glass hit the gravel and a spark was born. Instant bedlam erupted.

Graham was one of the regulars who spent Sunday mornings worshiping at Possum's drugstore, but he knew how unstable the pharmacist was and thought the shot was intended for him.

His car was in flames, but he ignored that small fact and pulled his pistol from his front pocket and fired back at Possum, knocking out both of the plate glass windows that occupied the space on either side of the drug store entrance. We never got an ice cream that afternoon.

I had learned long ago never to tell my mother any of the things I witnessed in town. We rode our mules back to the barn and she was home. "Hello. Tell your mother what you and your two friends have been doing."

"Nothing really," I answered. "We went to town, then we decided to ride back home. Wasn't anything happening in town."

"I see Alex brought those animals for you to ride. Your grandfather is getting much better, Luke. He actually asked if I minded you having that thing. Keep it out of the garden, though."

Chapter Eight

ETH CAME HOME FOR THE SUMMER, and me and Chilie met her at the train to bring her and her belongings home. She seemed excited to be home and spent the remainder of the day unpacking and chattering ninety to nothing. I sat on her bed and listened, responding to her hurried questions when asked. She had a dozen or so letters tied with a blue ribbon that she unpacked and carefully placed in the drawer of her night stand by her bed. The second she left the room on some errand downstairs I snatched the drawer open. The letters were addressed to her, and the return address was Reuben Squire's.

Things with the Taylor family assumed an uneasy peace. Cayro thought that all it would take for Bertram to be a good husband and father was that he be gainfully employed and feel that he contributed. I listened to Alex ranting sometimes, and became aware that the ugly truth was that Bertram liked the power he felt when he inflicted pain on other people. He even looked forward to the next time he could beat his wife and daughter without getting caught. He would have to be careful though. He had witnessed R. E. L. Carlton's legendary strength while working at the sawmill, and he didn't want to go in front of his boss, the mayor. He also didn't want to face Alex Campbell's angry fists either. He would bide his time, and when he got ready to leave this hick town again, he would tie up all the loose ends.

Becky grew taller than I was that summer, a fact that I secretly abhorred. Bertram started going to a beer joint named "Tumble Inn" every day after he got off work. Everyone said the place should be called "Stumble in, tumble out." Cayro and Becky were usually asleep before he got home. Cayro knew that her husband was like a volcano, ready to explode, but she kept hoping beyond hope that he would start acting right or leave again.

The war was over and the production lines that had turned out military vehicles for the war effort were now trying to meet a seemingly insatiable appetite for automobiles that a newly affluent buying public had. Pete signed up for a new Chevrolet. He parked the little convertible, that everyone in the county considered a lethal weapon, in the back side of the barn and told me that I could have it when I got big enough. When he got the shiny new car he didn't even come get me to take the first ride; he went by the pressing club and took Chilie. It hurt my feelings. I told him too.

Becky, Wash, and I kept the peanut stand open every morning that summer except Sundays. We picked plums and blackberries and sold them. We sold lemonade or Kool-Aid. We sold outgrown clothes and last year's pickles, and Mr. Weldon usually got our daily receipts. We always thought that he didn't like us until one day about mid-June. The three of us were inside his drug store pooling our money, trying to scrape together enough for an ice cream each and a comic book, when two farmers came in looking for the thin cotton gloves that they usually bought for the field hands to pull weeds from the crops. One man had a large red face with superficial blood vessels making a red road map on his nose and cheeks. He nodded in our direction in a friendly manner and told the accompanying farmer, "Wouldn't you like to have about twenty fine young folks like these to help pull weeds this summer?"

His unshaven, nasty-looking companion turned and looked at us and said, "I wouldn't let the sorry little bastards on my land."

Mr. Weldon's face turned red and his eyes bugged out. The blood vessels in the upper part of his face looked like blue worms under his skin before he blurted, "Shearer, you old, no-good, sleazy son of a bitch, who doesn't deserve the breath the Lord is letting you breathe, get out of my store and don't you ever insult another good customer of mine." After that, even if Possum would have been giving away triple dips we wouldn't have gone there. Mr. Weldon was our druggist. Eight flavors.

Dr. Ellis and a group of his fellow doctors scattered around the surrounding counties had formed a partnership several years before and had purchased the surrounding land south of Echowah Plantation and had dammed Echowah Creek in order to make a hydroelectric-generating plant. They foresaw the future and the growing demand for this mysterious source of energy, but they, like so many in their ranks, were brilliant, but had no common sense. Alex had warned him that he was getting in over his head, that generating electricity was simple; distribution was the problem. It made a fine place for the local people to fish but never made any money for the investors.

I rode with Alex one afternoon in late June to the dry-cleaning plant. It was on Saturday and the receipts for the week needed to be picked up. A wide counter, waist-high, separated the customer area from the back of the establishment. Six feet behind the counter was a partition wall that went from floor to ceiling and hid the working secrets of the dry-cleaning plant. In the past Alex would have let Mrs. Taylor take care of the receipts, but since his problem with her husband, he felt it incumbent to check on her physical well-being at least three times a week, a fact not left unnoticed by G. and R. gossip service, as Alex called them.

"Cayro, I mean, Mrs. Taylor, did you squeeze enough money out of the town people to make expenses this week?"

"We wouldn't have if Mary Louise hadn't sewn for the Proctor wedding coming up next month. People just don't seem to dry-clean as much in the summer time." She leaned across the counter and the bulges of her ample breasts could be seen under her thin cotton dress.

He wouldn't have cared if the weekly receipts had taken wing at that very moment and flown out the window. She knew he felt that way and he knew he felt that way and I knew he felt that way. A tiny smile played at the corners of her mouth and even at my tender age I knew trouble was on the way.

Miss Grace's two brothers were visiting for the week. The three of them had been born to a relatively well-off family, but when their parents died, the two boys left for Atlanta and the bright lights. In their later years the brothers came back occasionally to visit and brag about their accomplishments in the big city. They came to their hometown to visit their spinster sister in the early summer, and while they were here, they went fishing in the lake Doc Ellis and his buddies built. Miss Grace called Alex when the sheriff came to her door with his hat over his heart.

"Alex," the broken voice of the wailing Miss Grace said, "will you and Pete go down to the power plant and pick up my brothers? They drowned."

"Yes ma'am. I'll get them back to the funeral home as soon as I can drive down there and back. Clementine's going to insist on you seeing people from our house, so don't go to any trouble. You need the rest."

"You're a good man, Alex."

The main road from Chickasaw going south was called Killer's turnpike by the local people. It was dirt the entire thirty miles to the power dam. Chocolate-colored pebbles, a major component of the rich loamy earth south of town, made the road hazardous for high speeds in dry weather and slippery as eel crap in wet weather. Alex obviously didn't relish this assignment, so he asked Pete in the nicest tone he could muster, "Pete, do you think you could spare the time this afternoon to ride down to the power dam with me? Those two brothers of Miss Grace's drowned, and she asked if you and I would go get the bodies."

Pete eyed him suspiciously before asking the obvious, "You right sure she asked both of us to go?"

"Yep. Course now if you don't want to go, I can readily understand that. I used to be a bit squeamish about dead folks too."

"Are you going to buy the whiskey?"

"How much do you think it's going to take?"

"If it was me planning the trip I'd probably figure on a gallon or two."

"Let's see if O. Z. wants to go too. I'll go by Lonnie's and get enough for all of us."

When they got to the train station, Robert E. Lee Carlton was talking to Mr. Dean about shipping charges on a load of lumber he was sending to Atlanta. Pete stuck his head in the door and told O.Z. what their mission was and asked him if he wanted to go along. Mayor Robert E. Lee Carlton asked if he could go too. Alex went by Lonnie's again and the bootlegger shook his head as he watched them drive away. Mr. Dean said he couldn't understand why they were taking moonshine whiskey when Pete had almost a full case of good Canadian at the depot. Pete got mad with Mr. O. Z. and told him to keep his damned hands off his liquor.

"Pete, you know as good as I do that your main failing, other that being from the North, is your lack of self-discipline when it comes to hard liquor and the harsh principles that it maintains when it comes to violators of the rites of moderation. You don't have the proper respect for the stuff. I am, and I will continue to do so as long as I'm your friend, monitor your lack of willpower by keeping your source in check. Alex, will you pass the jug to the back seat please?"

When they arrived at the coroner's office in Bakertown to pick up the bodies, one empty gallon jug had been duly set on a fence post and shot at until Alex's pistol was empty. The jug could be used again, unscathed. Mayor Carlton was in the back seat, passed out. No one had put much thought into the problem of transporting two dead people in an automobile.

The only practical solution, as far as the non-comatose passengers could see, was to prop the mayor up in the corner of the back seat and sit the two corpses up in the seat with him. Alex put a gallon of Lonnie's finest, aged three weeks, between the mayor's feet and every time his honor made a sound someone would put the jug up to his lips. The other three sat in the front seat of the big car and argued about everything from who would win the next heavyweight title to who would win the next World Series, to who was going to have to fight the mayor when he woke up with the corpses.

The cold water used as a chaser for the strong liquor was gone. Alex decided to stop at Mr. Elidgah Price's farm to get some cold water. Lidge Price was an older planter who owned a large farm on the southern end of the county. He had turned most of the responsibilities of managing the big farm over to his only son, Coot, but he maintained a steady vigilance from one of the big rockers on the front porch.

Weather permitting, you could ride by the Price house any time of the day other than mealtime and Mr. Lidge would be rocking and staring. He was severely near-sighted and couldn't quite make out who was riding in the cars or trucks that passed his front porch, so he waved at every one who passed so as not to offend anyone. He had waved at the four as they passed earlier going south. "Why's that old man waving at us?" Pete had asked.

"He isn't an old man," quipped Mr. O. Z. "He happens to be the same age as me, and though I readily admit that I'm no spring chicken, I can hold my own with about anyone you can name. The fact is, if Alex hadn't taken Bertram to task, I was prepared to appoint myself to punish the man."

"The only thing you could beat is your damned gums."

They pulled up next to Mr. Lidge's mailbox, and Alex turned the engine off. He stepped from the driver's side and stood next to the front of the car. "Howdy, Mr. Lidge. Top of the afternoon to you."

"Who you be?" The old man squinted, trying to put the fuzzy image of the man with the voice.

"Alex Campbell here. Thought you might be interested in swapping a dipper of cold water for a drink of Lonnie's good 'shine whiskey."

"I imagine a swap could be arranged. Bring your jug and your friends, Alex, and visit awhile. How are things in the city. I don't go there much anymore since my eyes started failing me. Last time I drove I ran over one of James Jr.'s mules. The bastard had been out of the pasture for three or four days eating fresh clover off the side of the road. Busted my windshield and got mule shit all in my truck. I wish I hadn't opened my mouth to scream. You ever tasted mule shit, Alex?"

"No sir, can't say as I have. Mr. Lidge, you know O. Z. here. This other fellow is my Alex's father-in-law from Maine. Pete's his name."

The old man chuckled and said, "Well, I don't suppose we can hold being a Unionist against him forever, although I firmly believe that if they'd of had the cotton and we'd of had the guns the Confederate flag would be flying over the White House today."

"You could be right," Pete offered, then added, "What we never could understand was why you southerners fought so hard when you knew you couldn't win."

"Well, Pete, my grandpa told me they all thought y'all wanted our womenfolks. We never would have fought as hard if we'd of known that all y'all wanted was the slaves."

Pete didn't pursue the debate.

"Mammie. Whooop, Mammie," Mr. Lidge yelled as loud as he could, then spit a stream of Bloodhound chewing tobacco over the edge of the porch. Never a drop hit the porch. That was one thing that Mammie said that she would not clean up, and the tone of her voice told Mr. Lidge that she was dead serious about that.

"Yes sir, Mr. Lidge." A diminutive black woman, fully as old as Mr. Lidge, pushed the screen door partially open and answered the loud beckoning.

"These gentlemen have graciously proposed a swap of cool water for a portion of Lonnie's arthritis medicament. Since me and you both suffer from the debilitating disorder, I would suggest that one of us run along and fetch our end of the bargain. I'm already seated and entertaining our guests."

"Who would you suggest we send to the well, Mr. Lidge?"

"Dammit to hell, woman, I pay you three dollars a week to tend to me and I wind up waiting on you most of the time." A slight whine could be heard in his voice. Mr. Lidge's wife had died several years ago and he had come to rely on Mammie, their housekeeper for thirty years, to cook, clean house, and provide the limited amount of conversation that he required daily. Sadly now, she was getting too old to do much of anything. "If it wasn't for the bother of teaching somebody else all there is to do around here I'd find me a younger housekeeper...And one with a good figure." He added.

After he left to go get the cool water, she said, "If'n he didn't have nothing to complain about he'd dry up and blow away. My job is to give him something to live for, something to complain about all day."

He brought a galvanized tin bucket full of water, all that hadn't sloshed out, with two long-handled dippers sticking out of the bucket. He also brought a clean jelly jar so that he could pour Mammie a portion of the white "arthritis medicine."

The liquor had made its second round on the front porch when Mr. Lidge spotted the back seat occupants. "Who you got riding in the back seat of your car, Alex?"

"It's just Carlton and those two strange brothers of Miss Grace's."

"Carlton drunk?"

"As a skunk."

The gallon jug was passed around twice more and Mr. Lidge's voice was getting thick. "We ought to ask Miss Grace's brothers up on the porch, they look like they could stand a drink."

O. Z. stated for fact, "Lidge, those boys don't want a drink of liquor."

"They might not want a drink of liquor but they don't have to be so damned unsociable. Uppity as hell. That's what they are. They think 'cause they from Atlanta they better than us?"

Everyone sat on the porch rocking, except for the fuming Mr. Lidge. To him it was an insult for the two men to sit in the car and not accept his hospitality. He blurted, "Goddammit, they're going to have a drink with me. Just cause they're from Atlanta they act like they're better than the rest of us." He got out of his chair and walked two steps forward and two sideways and one step backwards toward the steps.

Pete made the attempt this time. "Mr. Lidge, those men simply want to be left alone. They don't mean to insult you."

He waddled over to the car and stuck his head in the back window. R. E. L. Carlton decided at that very moment to open one drunk eye. The face in the window was an obvious threat because it hadn't been there before, so he did what came natural to him and he hit the face in the window with a huge fist. The stunned Mr. Lidge backed his head out of the window and, holding his hand over an eye that was rapidly turning black, walked back to the porch and resumed his old seat in the rocker. "I guess you're right, those boys don't want to have a drink with us. Alex, would you mind terribly if I sent Mammie in the house to fetch my pistol? I've a notion to go out to your car and shoot Carlton."

"I couldn't let you do that, Mr. Lidge. He's a guest of mine."

"Then pass the jug, Alex."

My mother had the wake and the receiving of friends at our house for Miss Grace when they buried her brothers. Mr. Lidge didn't come but his son Coot did. Coot said his father's arthritis was much better thanks to Alex's arthritis medicine.

After the funeral me and Pete rode around the countryside. He was getting better at driving. I wasn't nearly as scared to ride with him now as I was when he first bought the car.

"Fine funeral, wasn't it?" he said absently.

"Yes sir. Reverend Cauley does a pretty good job of scaring me to death when he starts shouting about hell."

"That's the way he makes his living. Scaring the hockey out of the poor folks and the money out of the rich."

"Yes sir."

"Luke, do you ever talk to Mrs. Jackson? When you visit Wash does she ever talk about what she does or who she goes out with?"

"Pete, why don't you ask Mrs. Jackson out? We all know you're sweet on her."

"She wouldn't want to be seen with an old man like myself. She's more interested in younger men."

"You mean like Reuben Squire?"

He looked at me in a funny way then nodded his head. We drove the distance to our house in silence. I knew that he was thinking about Mrs. Jackson. Occasionally he would glance at himself in the rearview mirror as if to determine that he didn't look that old after all.

Cayro Taylor came to work on Monday, the day after Miss Grace's brothers had been buried, with two black eyes. Alex left the pressing club in a rage. He drove to Mayor Carlton's sawmill and confronted Bertram. "You don't have any right to beat helpless people."

"Mind your own business, Alex. What I do to my wife and daughter is nobody's business but mine."

"That's where you're wrong, Bertram. I'm issuing my final, and I mean my final, warning. If you lay a violent hand on either of them again I'll see you to hell."

"And if you threaten me again I'll meet you there."

"Bertram, I'm trying very hard to be right on this issue. No one has the right to beat people up simply because they feel like it. I'm not going to tell Carlton because you need the job." Alex walked away before the argument could escalate into an altercation that was unstoppable.

On Tuesday Mrs. Taylor told Alex that she appreciated his concern but asked him please not to interfere with Bertram anymore. She said that she and Becky had deserved the beating they got and she didn't want to give her husband a reason to get mad with them again.

Alex told her in the tenderest way, "Mary Louise, I had a man on my farm one time that sharecropped with me. He was probably the best farmer I ever had working my land. He made me good money every year. I saw him beating his mules one day, and he had a smile on his face. When we gathered the crop that fall I told him to leave. I don't know why I told you that story but one thing you can rest assured of, I'm not going to stand by and let any man, husband or not, beat you and Becky and let him smile when he does it."

"Alex, he's not going to quit. I don't mind him beating me, but when he beats Becky I can't bear it." She couldn't say anything further because of the tears of rage that stopped her voice.

"I'm not one to let another fight my battles or I'd tell Carlton and he would put him in jail. That would help for a while. Not long enough."

"Please don't."

"Cayro, If he beats you again, I'm going to stop him."

Chapter Nine

ME AND ALEX RODE TO TRINITY on Friday of that week. Trinity was the county seat of Chickasaw County, and it was always a thrill for me to go there. The town square was perfectly round and had concrete walks leading from the outer perimeter to the center. They resembled spokes on a wagon wheel. The entire area was splotched with large sugar maple, red maple, tulip poplar, hickory, and other hardwood that would make for a brilliant-colored fall foliage that had marked the coming home of the boys of summer, the summer soldiers who came home to a new south at the end of the Civil War. The Daughters of the Confederacy had planted the trees as a tribute to the brave men who marched home in 1865 when the forest bled the blood of October. In the center of the hub a cannon pointed north and a mounted Confederate officer high on a pedestal held his sword toward the north in a defiant gesture.

"What are we doing here, Alex?" I asked when we parked across the street from the courthouse in front of a lawyer's office.

The sign attached to the white clapboard wall of the small shotgun office proclaimed Paul and Paul, attorneys at law. Six steps led up to a small green porch. Gingerbread latticework framed the top of the porch columns and cross supports. "I've got to hire a lawyer."

"Why don't you get Colonel Jones? He lives down the street from us and you've always used him."

"This is a little different. I need someone who can get me out of trouble. These lawyers are the best in the county at that."

The small anteroom where I sat waiting for Alex's appointment to be over had a small couch and matching chair. A receptionist sat behind a small desk filing her nails and looking bored. I sat on the couch trying to look bored. Today was Friday and she glanced at the wall clock through teardrop-shaped glasses. She had escorted Alex to the office behind the reception area and had left the door slightly cracked so that she could listen to the privileged information in the inner office. I could hear better than she.

I heard Alex raise his voice. "Listen, I didn't come over here for advice about what I shouldn't do. All I want to know is if you can get me out of trouble if I shoot the son of a bitch!"

"It will take a lot of money," one of the Pauls replied.

"I'll pay you the standard rate on an hourly basis. Not one cent more. Don't try to suggest otherwise. Now I'm not a mushroom. I don't like the dark or bullshit. If you want the goddam job, let me know this instant."

A smile played on the receptionist's face, and it crossed my mind that she really didn't like her bosses very much. She enjoyed listening to them getting fussed at.

The green park benches were filling up with afternoon loafers and strollers as we turned around the square headed for home. I asked him, "Alex, what you going to do? You're not going to leave us, are you?"

"No, Luke. If there's any justice anywhere I won't have to go. The thing that bothers me most is the failure of the system. It seems that if you're looking for a screwing you go to the courthouse and if you want justice you go to the whorehouse."

"And you're going to the courthouse."

"You're a smart boy, Luke."

The trip home was quiet. I thought of all the ominous things that could possibly happen. I had lived most of my life without a father and I didn't understand what was going on, but I didn't want to be without my grandfather.

Mayor Carlton stopped by the pressing club on Friday. He was a devoutly Christian man most of the time. His detours from the heavenly path occurred mostly under the influence of strong drink. He had promised the Lord years before when he was destitute that he would give the church its due if only the Lord would let him make some money. When his tenacity and hard work paid off and he began to make money, he gave the church his tithe. He always got one of his two suits dry-cleaned before he sat on the front bench of First Baptist and nodded and snored on Sunday mornings. He saw the bruises on Cayro Taylor's neck and face and drove to his sawmill and fired Bertram.

Saturday morning Doctor Ellis set Cayro Taylor's broken arm. Sister Ruby saw her walk down the street to the drugstore to get her prescription filled. She saw the cast and assumed the rest. By lunch she had made her regular gossip rounds via the telephone.

Me, my mother, Alex, and Pete sat down to a noon dinner of fresh garden vegetables and pork chops prepared by my mother. I had made plans the day before with Becky and Wash to walk over to Bryant's crossroads to pick plums and blackberries to sell at our peanut stand. Wash walked in unannounced and without speaking and sat at a the far end of the dinner table.

"Would you care for some lunch?" my mother asked Wash.

"Done ate. Thank you just the same, Miss Clem."

"Do you want some peach pie while you wait on Luke?"

"I ain't ate that much. Do you reckon there would be ice cream on the peach pie?"

"Where's Becky?" I asked when my mother had gone for Wash's pie.

"She can't come. Her mama's got a broke arm."

I noticed Alex had stopped eating and was listening to Wash.

"How did she break her arm?" I asked.

"Mr. O. Z. said he saw Bertram coming from Lonnie's house with a package. He said Bertram probably did it. Becky wouldn't open the screen door when I went by to get her."

My mother was in the kitchen getting Wash's peach pie and ice cream. When she came back to the dining room, Alex had left the room.

"Where's your grandfather?" She saw his half-eaten meal, and concern clouded her features. "What did you tell him?"

"Wash told him about Bertram breaking Mrs. Taylor's arm."

Her face turned white and she ran through the house calling for Alex. When she opened the front door, Alex was driving down the drive toward town. She returned to the dining room and addressed her father. "Will you please see if you can find Mr. Campbell? I'm afraid."

Pete saw the concern on his daughter's face and left the table. My mother called the Taylor residence and I'm sure Sister Ruby listened in on the conversation. I listened, suddenly not hungry anymore, to her side of the conversation. When she hung up the phone, she said to no one, "Thank goodness he's not at home. Maybe Alex won't find him until he cools off."

When Alex didn't come back in a reasonable amount of time, my mother sent Wash home and she, Pete, and I sat in the front room waiting.

Alex came home an hour later. Beth and my mother met him at the door and studied his face for an answer.

"Carlton and the sheriff got him before I could find him. He stole one of Carlton's lumber trucks and drove it out to the farm and set fire to two of my barns. I filed charges against him and Carlton filed charges. The sheriff talked to the judge after Bertram signed a confession. Judge Greer said he'd make sure Bertram didn't breathe a free breath for the next twenty years." The women sat and sighed with relief.

Cayro Taylor filed for a divorce the following Monday, but southern protocol dictated that she publicly hold the persons responsible for her husband's incarceration in disdain, so a new field of play was established. She treated Alex thusly.

On Saturday Pete, Mr. O. Z., and Alex went fishing while Chilie drove me and my mother to the county seat to shop. I didn't want to go, but she stated that she wasn't about to buy clothes for me without me being there to try them on. When we got back late that afternoon there was a note taped to the mirror of the hall tree. Beth's crisp, neat handwriting declared that she had eloped with Reuben Squire and would get the remainder of her things the following week.

When Alex and Pete got home, my mother sent me to my room, but I still heard Alex shouting and the walls were thick and well built.

Reuben didn't come with Beth when she came for her things the next week. Beth was radiant and obviously happy, but she stayed silent as she waited for her father's response and grudgingly given approval. He just stood there looking at her with a strange expression.

"Be happy for me, Daddy. I love him very much, and he loves me."

I saw a tear forming in Alex's eye, then he opened his arms and he and Beth made their peace.

"Ask Reuben if he minds coming by to see me tomorrow morning. It's time I talked to my son-in-law." The words seemed to choke Alex.

I had no doubt that I would be sent out of the room if Reuben called, so I rose early and watched each morning. Three days later, when I saw Reuben's car pull in the drive, I ran to the coat closet in the parlor and waited. It wasn't long before I heard Alex's strong voice. "Come on in the sitting room, Reuben. Have a seat. I don't believe in beating around the bush. I want to tell you up front that I don't approve of this marriage and for that matter I don't approve of you, but it seems we're stuck with each other, so I'm offering a peaceful coexistence."

Reuben laughed easily, and said, "Campbell, peace is boring. What is it you wanted to talk to me about?"

"Well. There's nothing like getting off on the right foot. I guess the only thing I've got to say is that she's the only child I've got, Reuben, and I won't have her mistreated. If you get tired of her, send her home but don't mistreat her."

"Campbell, let me explain something to you. She belongs to me now and I'll do whatever the hell I want to. Don't worry though. I wouldn't hurt a hair on her head. She's very special."

I heard Alex suck his breath in, but he kept his voice low. "Reuben, I don't have a good feeling about this, but I'm glad you feel that way. I'm willing to accept this and welcome you to the family."

Reuben left without responding, and I thought I would wet my pants before Alex finally quit pacing and swearing and left the room.

Things were bad in the beginning, and they got worse. Beth called almost every day, but her conversations were stilted and sometimes ended abruptly. My mother called her often, and sometimes she ended the conversation with a puzzled look as the line went dead.

Beth was mentally fragile, a fact acknowledged by everyone in the family but never mentioned. Everyone suspected that she could be pushed past the point of acceptable mental tolerances that a stronger person could endure. Beth had been raised almost without the benefit of a mother, and she had responded to the loud world by withdrawing. Her quietness had been interpreted as aloofness, but the truth was, she was shy to the point of preferring to withdraw into her own silent world rather than be pulled into the boisterous world that Alex favored.

Two months passed, and Beth visited us just three times. Each time you could tell that she was deteriorating both physically and mentally. Alex talked to her earnestly and lovingly. He seemed to dwindle physically when she would leave. He was caught in a quagmire. He couldn't go after Reuben and alienate Beth, and he couldn't just stand by and watch her shrivel up.

An uneasy time settled over our house. Alex didn't talk unless it was necessary. In fact he avoided any unnecessary contact with anyone so he wouldn't have to respond. He left early each morning and stayed gone much of the day. He rode to Reuben and Beth's house each day until Beth asked him to please stop checking on her.

The first Saturday in August it all came to an end. The day started in a way typical of all dog days. Hot and muggy. By noon a haze had dimmed the normally blue sky, the dogs took refuge in shady places, and the birds stayed unstirred and left the sky unmarked. Only the insects flourished. I stayed down by the barn most of the morning and out of the silence of our house, a silence that shouted that something was amiss. I fed our mules, now seldom ridden, and watched them lazily flick their long tails at bothersome horseflies when they bit. Watching from behind the three tails flicking incessantly was almost hypnotic. At lunch I heard Lucy calling and slowly walked to our house.

After I said grace and after the necessary exchange of small talk involving the various dishes of the meal, Alex settled into his usual silence. The telephone rang from the front room, and my mother, who seemed relieved that she had some small task to do, rose to answer.

A half-minute passed, and she opened the door leading to the dining room. "Dr. Ellis needs to speak to you, Alex. I told him you were eating lunch, but he insisted."

My mother forsook good manners and followed Alex back into the parlor. In a matter of seconds she hurriedly came back to where Pete and I waited. "Drive me down to Dr. Ellis's please, Father. Beth has been in some sort of accident. I don't think he would tell Mr. Campbell anything except that she was in bad shape."

No one questioned me, so I hopped in the back seat and held on as Pete tore down the street toward town.

Beth was barefoot, and her dress was soiled and torn. She had a faraway look on her face as she stared straight ahead, her eyes clear but unblinking. Dried blood had trailed down from her mouth and nose and had stained the white collar of her summer dress. Old brown bruises and new blacker ones were on her face, neck, and arms. When we had gotten there, Alex was desperately trying to get her to speak to him, but she only stared as if he didn't exist. Alex pleaded with her, his voice strange-sounding and tears flowing down his face, but she remained silent. Dr. Ellis had stood silently, holding her hand since we arrived, with a look of impending doom on his face.

What seemed to be a long time passed, with Alex and my mother speaking low to Beth and getting no response. Dr. Ellis cleaned the blood away and applied an ointment to the cuts on her face. My mother retrieved a brush from her purse and brushed Beth's hair back and secured it with a small ribbon she fished from the ample purse. Alex stood there, stooped and looking very old and tired. I guess an hour must have passed when Dr. Ellis spoke: "Alex, you might as well take Beth home. My medicine isn't strong enough to heal her wounds."

Alex straightened. He escaped from some deep thought he was having and shook his head. "I guess you're right, Doc.

Her hurt is inside somewhere. Did Reuben say anything when he brought her by?"

Dr. Ellis hesitated, then he cleared his throat loudly. He looked Alex squarely in the eye. "Reuben didn't bring her in. That oldest Morgan boy passed her walking toward town. He was so upset I sent him home."

Alex didn't seem terribly upset, or if he was, he hid it well. I expected him to blow up and was admittedly a little disappointed when he didn't. The fact is that Pete and my mother seemed madder at Reuben than Alex did. I should have known better.

We all helped to get Beth's limp body up to her old room. When she felt her old familiar bed, her lips moved almost imperceptibly as if she were trying to smile, and she closed her eyes and immediately went to sleep. We all sat and watched her for a while, then Alex excused himself and said he needed to stretch his legs for a few minutes. Everyone stood and walked to the window when we heard Alex's car start. My mother looked anxiously at Pete, then the door opened and Lucy's words turned my mother's anxiety into panic.

"He got his pistol out of the hall chest." Lucy was half-crying.

Pete left to see if he could find Alex, and my mother ran to the phone and finally got the chief of police on the phone. Sister Ruby listened.

"If you see Mr. Campbell, will you please stop him? I'm afraid he's going to kill someone or get killed himself."

Pete drove up at three o'clock and told us he had ridden everywhere that he could think Reuben might be and he didn't see either man. We sat in the parlor and waited silently.

At four that afternoon Alex drove slowly down the long drive and stopped the car in front of the house. He left the door open as if he would be back soon.

When he opened the front door and saw us sitting in the front room, a sad smile appeared for a brief moment. My mother looked up wistfully at Alex, hoping for the best but knowing that something was irreversibly wrong. I had no earthly idea why I had been sequestered, but when he finally spoke I felt a cold wind blow through the room. "Pete," he said, "do you think you can drive me over to Trinity. I need to talk to the sheriff."

My mother rose from her chair and walked to Alex silently. She put her arms around his neck and cried softly.

When several minutes passed, he gave her his handkerchief and said, "Clemmy, do you mind packing my toilet articles and a few changings? I may be gone for a while. Is Beth talking now?"

"Can I go with you and Pete to Trinity?" I asked.

Alex looked away from my mother, who was openly crying. "It would be a special favor to me, Clemmy, if you'd let mine and Pete's grandson go with us. I'm going upstairs and spend a little time with Beth, then we'll go."

Alex came down about an hour later. I knew he had tried to talk to Beth, but I knew she wasn't ever going to talk again.

The sheriff's office was located in the front of the gray painted, brick, jail. The night jailer had two tiny rooms on the second floor. All county prisoners were locked in eight-by-twelve cells on the bottom floor immediately behind the sheriff's office. I sat in the outer room on a half couch alone as Alex and Pete went into the private office. Sheriff Gaines was a big man and his voice matched his statue. I could plainly hear his side of the conversation. "Goddammit, Alex, why did you kill the son of a bitch? God knows he deserved it, but I've got to charge you. Why didn't you put a knife in the bastard's hand? Goddammit, Alex, this is an election year and I've got all the problems a man ought to have. Didn't he threaten you?"

"Henry, I did what I would do if I had seen a dog with rabies, now charge me with whatever you must. I knew what I was doing. I shot the son of a bitch. If I told anybody it was self-defense they wouldn't believe me. You don't … I brought you my pistol."

"Alex," the sheriff pleaded, "in the state of Georgia first-degree murder carries the penalty of death by electrocution. Goddammit."

Pete intervened, "Gaines, I'm not overly familiar with the laws in Georgia, but in Maine they shake a man's hand when he kills a varmint."

"Well, they don't here. They ought to, but they don't. What they are going to do is electrocute you, Alex. That's what they're going to do. And the voters will blame me. Goddammit. All I ever wanted to be was sheriff."

Chapter Ten

THE SHERIFF WAS QUIETER NOW. "Alex, I'm going to have to keep you until Monday morning. Then we'll see if the judge decides whether you're bondable or not. I would call him now, but today being Saturday, I know he ain't sober at the moment. I'm going to call Lizzy and tell her to fix up the guest room. The law don't say where the sheriff has to keep a prisoner, so I guess you can stay at my house until Judge Greer sobers up."

The bond hearing was set by Judge Greer that Monday for the following morning at ten o'clock. I knew better than to ask my mother if I could go with her and Pete. I pretended that I wasn't listening to them at breakfast that Tuesday when they absently talked about what Pete should wear and what time they should leave. When breakfast was over, I excused myself, and as an afterthought said, "Do you care if Wash comes over and plays with me while you are gone?"

She looked at me in a peculiar way because she knew that Wash would show up anyway whether asked or not. "Luke, is anything wrong with you?" What puzzled her was why I hadn't asked to go.

"No, ma'am."

I waited in the kitchen until they went upstairs to get dressed. Then I ran to my room and put on church clothes. I wet my hair and plastered it down as best as I could. Then I went back through the kitchen and on to the barn where Pete kept his automobile. I lay on the back floorboard for close to an hour under an old mothball-smelling blanket before I heard one door open and shut, then the other door opened and slammed hard. That would be Pete. "He must have walked to meet Wash," I heard my mother say.

"Clementine, you worry too much about that boy. He's resourceful enough to take care of himself. I wonder why he didn't pitch a fit to go with us?"

"I suppose it was because he knew that I wouldn't allow him to. Alex is not a criminal and I certainly won't be a party to exposing my son to seeing him treated like one."

"Nobody is going to treat him like a common criminal. I don't care that much for Alex, but if anyone treated him badly they would have to answer to me."

"I don't know when you two are going to stop acting like you hate each other. You are both very nice men and I love both of you, but I swear sometimes I think Luke has more sense." Her voice broke and she continued as she softly cried. "Why in the name of God did he kill the man?"

It took thirty minutes to drive to the county seat. My left side was beginning to get numb, and I itched on every square inch of my body. When the car finally stopped and both doors slammed shut I snatched the blanket off and sat up rubbing my numb arm. I watched as they crossed the street and disappeared through the doors of the red brick courthouse. When the big

Chapter Ten

clock on top of the courthouse started bonging ten o'clock I ran across the street and went through the same doors. A black man wearing a white and blue prisoner's suit was slowly sweeping the black and white tiles that covered the big hall. Spittoons were stationed by each of the several glass-fronted doors that were equally spaced on each side of the long hall. At the far end of the wide hall stairs led to the second floor. I walked to the prisoner and cleared my throat. Already looking for any excuse to stop sweeping he looked down and said, "Anyway I can help you? You wouldn't happen to have a spare smoke on you, would you?"

"No sir, I don't smoke. Can you tell me where the judge holds bond hearings?"

He pointed to the end of the hall where the stairs were located. "Up them eighteen steps is where his honor presides but he ain't there yet and drunk or not I ain't never known him to be late."

"Is there anywhere I can go, to listen to what's going on, without going in the room they're in?"

"At the top of the stairs before you go into the main court-room is a set of stairs that go on up to the balcony. You can go up there and nobody but the lawyers and the judge can see you. You sure you ain't got something to smoke?"

The judge's bench was elevated two steps above the raised platform that filled the front of the courtroom. Twelve comfortable-looking seats were behind a waist-high banistered fence on the left side of the judge's bench. An equal number of seats were on the right side, and Alex, the sheriff, the two lawyers Alex had hired, and three deputies sat on that side and talked in low tones. From the sounds of the whispers and coughs under the balcony there must have been quite a few spectators. I knew that Pete and my mother were under there somewhere. I knew she was crying.

A large round clock hung high on the wall above the judge's bench. It proclaimed to the courtroom that the time was fifteen after ten. The door to the right of the bench opened and the Honorable Jackarius J. Greer entered suffering from a massive hangover. His skin was almost blue except for his red bulbous nose. The sheriff jumped to his feet and said in a loud voice, "All rise."

Judge Greer stumbled up to his seat and sat down. The sheriff said equally loud, "You may be seated."

The judge banged his gavel on the podium and said, "I fine myself one hundred dollars for being late to court. Sheriff, you may collect the fine when this hearing is over. I'm also going to sentence myself to thirty days at the county work camp with these days to be spent on probation. I consider myself sufficiently remorseful for being late. This hearing is now in session."

The sheriff stood up and told the court, "This hearing is to determine if one Alex Campbell, one now charged with first-degree murder in the county of Chickasaw, state of Georgia, is eligible for bond. What say you?"

I watched and listened to the proceedings, not understanding all that happened but able to grasp the general flow. The lawyers representing Alex paraded at least twenty character witnesses to the witness stand to attest to the general goodness of Alex. A few minutes before noon, the judge looked at his watch and said, "Are there any present who wish to attest to the bad character of Mr. Campbell? I'm going to make my decision at twelve o'clock." He nodded in the direction of Alex's lawyers and said, "No need in you parading any more witnesses up here. I've known Alex about as long as anybody in this room and I've agonized over this thing since I heard about it, but statutes of the state of Georgia limit how far I can stretch the arm of justice." He looked hard at Alex then continued. "Alex, are you absolutely certain that the man didn't impose a threat to your physical well-being?" Alex shook his head, and a muted "No" could be heard from the lower gallery.

At exactly twelve noon the judge banged his gavel and proclaimed, "The prisoner will approach the bench. I'm sorry, Alex, but this is a court of law, and I've got to call you a prisoner."

"I understand, your honor."

"I'm stretching the limits of the law, but you haven't pled your case yet so I'm going to assume that you might be convicted of justifiable homicide. Alex, bear in mind that if you come back to this court and you plead first-degree murder, then I have no choice but to sentence you to the electric chair." He waited for a long time, looking at the ceiling, then the balcony, then he looked at me. He motioned for the sheriff and whispered something to him then continued. "I'm going to set the bond for fifty thousand dollars cash. Is anyone present who will post the bond?" A general gasp came from the onlookers because of the amount of the bond and the stipulation that it be paid in cash.

I heard Pete's angry voice from under the balcony. "If your honor will allow me to wire the money into the bail bond account I'll have it transferred by noon tomorrow."

A deputy came to the balcony and asked what I was doing there. It scared me so that I cried out and Alex looked up and saw me. Boy, was I ever going to catch hell when we got home.

Alex came home the next day, and I heard him tell Lucy, "That tall Swede the sheriff is married to was going to kill me with her cooking before the state got its chance."

Me and Wash walked to Mr. Weldon's drugstore for some ice cream two days after Reuben Squire's funeral and the day after the bond hearing. In a small town the funeral is held mostly for the benefit of the dead person's family. If Reuben had been without family no one in town would have gone, but Reuben's old parents had many friends. Two older ladies of obvious wealth were sitting at one of the small chrome and artificial granite topped tables. I heard the lady with the blue hair ask her companion, "Darling, did you go to Reuben's funeral?"

Her friend answered, "I did. I wouldn't have gone if it weren't for Mrs. Squire."

"Nor I."

"Didn't you think that Reverend Cauley did an excellent job conducting the funeral service?"

"Considering the raw material the preacher had to work with, he did the best he could do."

"I agree. Did an excellent job in fact. Reuben would stymie the imagination of sweet Jesus himself trying to come up with something good to say about him."

Mrs. Blue Hair asked, "What do you think is going to happen to Alex Campbell?"

"My George says that Alex will go to the electric chair over in Reidsville. He's getting up a petition signed by all the members of our country club asking the governor to pardon Alex. George and the governor were fraternity brothers."

All at once I felt like I was going to throw up, and I saw black spots in front of my eyes. Mr. Weldon had been listening to the ladies talking and watching me at the same time. I remember his fat white arms reaching for me where I had sat on the floor. He said over and over as he carried me to his car, "There now Luke, don't cry no more. We aren't going to let anyone hurt your granddaddy."

I hadn't seen Becky since Alex got her daddy put in jail. I thought it was time, so Wash and I walked to her house the next morning. I said, "Becky, me and Wash and Mr. Weldon miss you. Can you start coming with us again?"

"I already asked my mama. She said I couldn't for a while."

"But ..."

"Maybe I can slip out tomorrow."

We left, and I told Wash I was still going to marry Becky. "Not me," he said. "I'm going to get my mule when I'm old enough and ride to Montana and be a cowboy. Women are too much damned trouble."

"I might go with you. Do you think we might really get to be cowboys?"

"Probably so, but I think I'd rather be a train robber. They make more money."

I thought that things as I had known them would never be the same again, that the normal was forever replaced with things alien, things strange. Alex didn't bounce into the dining room for breakfast as he once did. Conversation that had once bordered on good-natured argument between him and Pete was subdued. My mother often left the table in tears. Preacher Cauley came by our house late one day and managed an invitation to stay for supper.

When we had all sat down to the good-smelling meal my mother and Lucy had prepared, Preacher Cauley was called on to say grace. "Dear Lord, I call on you this night to bless this food to give us sustenance and strength in order to serve thy wishes and to offer good will to our fellow man. Lord, I realize that when you sent Moses down the mountain of Sinai with your commandments that you meant for us to keep them. Lord, Brother Alex has broke one of your commandments, but I ask you to forgive him because the man needed killing. Now if you'll forgive me for rushing this prayer, this fine supper is getting cold. Amen."

I looked at my mother, and she was smiling, then giggling. Pete was turning an odd shade of purple and looked as if he were on the verge of exploding, which he did. Laughter erupted from him like I had never heard before. Alex was slapping his hands on the table and whooping like a crane. My mother had her napkin over her mouth trying unsuccessfully to stifle her laughter. Even Preacher Cauley laughed loudly. After several attempts to stop laughing my mother choked out, "Preacher, we were trying to keep the Lord from hearing about this." Another round of loud laughing took the adults. I never understand what was funny. My chicken and mashed potatoes was getting cold and that certainly wasn't funny.

After the meal Alex trudged up the stairs, as he did after every meal, to be with Beth for a while. She still stared at nothing. I went with my mother or Lucy most times when they fed her. She wasn't going to come out of the shell it didn't seem.

The next morning Alex and Pete rode to Dr. Ellis's and sold him the laundry. My mother said it was "protocol." People might not do business with the laundry any more since Alex got in trouble. I was beginning to agree with Wash, and the lure of the cowboy's life made more and more sense. I didn't want to ride my old mule all the way to Montana though. Maybe I could weasel a horse from Alex or Pete for my birthday.

After several days of moping around the house and garden I could tell that Alex was getting restless. I knew something was bothering him a great deal and I thought I knew what it was. I heard him tell Chilie one morning after breakfast, "Get the car out and clean it up, Chilie. The mountain won't come to me so I'm going to have to go to the mountain."

"What you mean is that you're going to go over to Mrs. Taylor's house."

"Damn you, Chilie, how can you read my mind like you do?"

"You talk to yourself a heap, Mr. Alex. I just listen in on the conversation."

Chilie told me later that Alex had him stop at Mr. O. Z.'s house. Chilie asked him, "What we going to do here, Mr. Alex? You know Mr. O. Z. is at the depot."

"I'm just going to borrow something, Chilie."

Chilie told me later, "He came back with a handful of big red roses from Mr. O. Z.'s back yard, and I drove him straight to Miss Cayro's house. He knocked on the door, and she came to the door but wouldn't let him in. She kept the screen door fastened. Mr. Alex had his hat over his heart and was talking real earnest-like and I couldn't hear a word neither one of them said no matter how hard I tried even though I strained my ear pans to the limit. After a while she opens the screen door and takes the roses and I heard him tell her, 'I'll see you over in Trinity, Saturday afternoon.'"

Wash started going by and getting Becky and then the two of them would ride their bikes to a designated place where I would be waiting. We didn't hide being together around town, and soon the town people forgot that we were supposed to be awkward around each other. Mrs. Taylor, I suspected, knew that Becky was spending time with me and Wash but she didn't delve and Becky didn't volunteer.

The summer turned into a real hellfire scorcher. The three of us rode to the pond almost every afternoon and swam in the pool in our underwear. Chilie caught us swimming, but I knew that he wouldn't tell. He and I had a good understanding. He didn't tell on me and I didn't tell Alex about him taking Alex's car and riding his women around in it. Alex thought that car got awful gas mileage.

Becky never mentioned her father, but she had never talked about him before he went to prison either.

One day in July we parked our bikes and walked around the cabin to the pool. Strange sounds came from the tall grass and trees. A kind of clacking, singing sound, totally indescribable. Big gray insects with gossamer wings floated on the water. I had never heard any sound like we were hearing now and I had never seen any insect that resembled these strange big things. When we started home I put one in my shirt pocket. That night at the supper table I remembered and showed the insect to the three at the table. "What is this?" I asked.

Alex looked at the insect and said, "According to Greek legend the gods got angry with a village and turned all the people into these cicadas and made them sing their lives without stopping until they died. The gods could have given them a more pleasant voice though."

"How come I never have seen them or heard them before now?"

"It's because they only come out of the ground every so many years and sprout wings and sing."

"How many years?" I asked.

"You're a smart boy, you figure it out. I'm fifty-one now. I've heard the cicadas song four times in my life. When they sing five times I'll probably be dead of old age. The first time I heard them I was eleven."

I figured and finally said, "They sing every thirteen years."

"Well, I'll be doggone. I suppose that's why they're called thirteen-year cicadas."

"You aren't going to be dead of old age when you're sixty-five." My mother interjected.

"I think you're right, Clementine. I think something else might do it."

Slowly the town found other tongue-wagging fodder. The first few weeks after the killing the subject of Alex's sin took precedence even over the weather. Everybody knew it was hot and everybody knew that we needed rain, but a previously unheard tidbit concerning the shooting was a nugget that needed immediate airing. The common prelude by the teller of the gossip would most assuredly instruct the avid listener. "Now you can't tell a soul what I'm going to tell you." This assured the silence of the listener for a precious little time to give the bearer of the gossip time to break his story to someone else.

Mayor Carlton got drunk and visited every store in town. He told each proprietor that enough was enough and for each to warn his customers that he was going to beat the hell out of any man he heard say another word about his friend Alex. Nobody said anything else in front of the Mayor.

The September term of court was six weeks away. Alex's case was on the docket. Civil court would be for the first two days then the criminal docket would be heard. Alex would plead guilty to first-degree murder and place his hands at the mercy of the court unless someone could convince him to lie and say that it was self defense.

Chapter Eleven

*L*IFE WAS ABNORMALLY NORMAL, except for the gloom that settled over me whenever I thought of Alex going to the electric chair. Mary Louise Jackson stopped me in town one day when the weather was normal and hot as hell and she asked if Pete ever asked about her.

"No, ma'am, but that don't mean anything. Pete wouldn't ask me anything about you anyway."

"Do you think he's still mad with me for dancing with Reuben Squire at that stupid dance?"

"I think he got real upset when you had a date with Reuben last Christmas. Him and Alex got into several cussing contests after that night. He even cussed Chilie out and Chilie hadn't done anything. He even cussed the cat out. I don't think he ever got over you going with Reuben."

She smiled in an impish way and swished toward the laundry. She said over her shoulder as she stepped from the flagstone sidewalk into the street. "Luke, tell your grandfather that it's important that I see him this afternoon."

"You're going with me to the laundry," he ordered when I told him at lunch that Mrs. Jackson needed to see him.

We drove to the pressing club after stopping and picking up Wash who was on his way to our house. "Where're y'all going?"

"Your mama wanted to talk to Pete, so we're going by there."

"You have any idea what she might want with me, Wash?"

"Yes sir."

"Well."

"Well what, Mr. Pete?"

Pete wanted to shout but couldn't. "Can you tell me what she wants?"

"No sir."

Now Pete really wanted to shout now, but he didn't. "Why in the name of h... . Why can't you tell?"

"Because she told me she would beat my butt good if I said anything."

We followed Pete through the open, full-paned double doors that let in customers and what sparse breeze that hot August day could muster. Even though the temperature was hotter in the building than it was outside, neither Mrs. Taylor nor Mrs. Jackson showed any signs of heat discomfort. When Mrs. Jackson came to the front of the store and leaned on the chest-high counter, an almost imperceptible line of perspiration was on her upper lip. When she saw Pete she smiled prettily and said, "Hello, Pete. It's been a long time since you've come in."

He mumbled something about helping Alex and looked thoroughly uncomfortable.

"I'll come right to the point. My cousin is getting married in Macon this Saturday and the reception is Saturday night. I would like for you to be my escort. Plan on staying the night if you can go. If you need your good suit pressed, you should bring it back this afternoon." She looked him in the eye, then slightly licked her lower lip and smiled sweetly.

Pete was completely flabbergasted. He said on the way to the door, "I'll have to think about it, what I mean is I'll have to see what my schedule is." He stopped before he reached the doors and turned around and stuck his jaw out. "Yes ma'am, I'd be honored to take you to that wedding. Wash, Luke, let's go over to Trinity. I've been needing a new suit anyway." He stepped quicker to his car than I'd seen him in months.

Coming back from Trinity late that afternoon, Wash said, "Mr. Pete would you pick another tune to whistle? You've been whistling that same one over and over all afternoon and it's getting to wear thin."

Queen Ester was Lucy's best friend and her Aunt to boot. They were exactly the same age, in fact Lucy was born two days before her Aunt. While Wash's mama was gone with Pete to Macon he was staying with me. Queen Ester came by our house that Saturday to visit with Lucy and while she was there told her that if we wanted to come, bring me and Wash with her tomorrow afternoon to the barbecue at Antioch A.M.E. Church. The sheriff wasn't the only one facing reelection this year. The governor of Georgia was running for reelection. He had served as governor for one year after the last governor, his father, died in office. Georgia law wouldn't allow but one four-year term as governor, but this was the exception. Now he wanted to run for a full term. He was going to speak to the black churchgoers tomorrow afternoon, and a free barbecue ensured that a big crowd would be there. No one knew or cared that the barbecues that the campaigning governor held at the black churches on Sundays were what was left over from the Saturday meetings he held with the white voters.

He was a pure politician. At the white churches and clubs he would pop his red suspenders and proclaim to the crowd that he didn't need nor did he want any black folks to vote for him. At the black churches he would pop his red suspenders and say how much he would spend on black schools and colleges if he were sent back to the state capitol.

Since we were going to church, I didn't see any need to gain my mother's permission. Me and Wash asked Lucy if we could go and if we could take Becky with us. Lucy and Queen Ester agreed to that.

That afternoon Becky met us at Mr. Weldon's drugstore. I got the longest straw when me and Wash pulled it and I would be the one to tell her. "Guess what!" I said. "Me and you and Wash get to go meet the governor tomorrow. We can go with Lucy to her church where he's going to speak."

"Does your mother know about this?"

Wash interrupted, "You know damn well his mother don't know. We ain't never told any of our mothers what we was doing. What's that got to do with you going or not?"

"If y'all are going then I'm going too."

That settled, we turned to more pressing affairs, trying to scrape up enough money for three ice creams. We had two pennies left over so we asked Mr. Weldon if he could give each of us a little extra ice cream. He said hell no and don't ever ask him again then he threw his fat arms up in the air and said.

"You three are going to be the reason for my early demise." He gave us all an extra full scoop.

The church meeting we were going to with Lucy started at three that Sunday. My mother had made me and Wash go with her to Sunday school and regular church service. Mrs. Taylor had started going to the Methodist church after what had happened because all of us except Pete went to the Baptist church. When Pete went at all he went to the Catholic church in Trinity. I heard him tell Chilie one day about the last time he had gone to confession. He told Chilie he started confessing and when the Priest had dropped his bible the fourth time he didn't confess any more of his sins.

We were walking home from church on one side of the street and Mrs. Taylor and Becky were walking home from the Methodist church on the other side. She and my mother exchanged polite nods then continued. Becky waved and me and Wash waved back. We all had to keep on our church clothes if we were going with Lucy and that wouldn't be easy.

At lunch my mother was preoccupied and didn't seem to notice that me and Wash hadn't changed clothes yet. She absently said several times, "I guess daddy and Mrs. Jackson will be getting home before too much longer." Then she would sigh and move her food around the plate with her fork, never eating anything. Once she thought she heard a car drive up and she went to the window and looked out. Me and Wash excused ourselves and went to my room to wait until she would be in the kitchen cleaning up and couldn't see us leave.

At 2:30 Chilie picked me, Wash, and Becky up at the park. The center of the small park was occupied by a gazebo-type bandstand with wooden benches stretched between each upright support except for an opening on the four corners.

It was here that we had patiently waited trying not to soil our Sunday clothes. Chilie drove to Lucy's and picked her and Queen Ester up and we sped off to the church.

Lucy yelled at Chilie above the wind noise from four down windows. "Chilie, slow this car down, you know I'm afraid of high speeds."

"Miss Lucy, I ain't driving but forty-five."

"That's too fast for me."

"Aw, Miss Lucy, if I don't hurry all the ribs is going to be ate up, and all the single women's going to be already spoke for."

The church yard was full when we got there. Mules and wagons were tied for several hundred yards on either side of the road and out numbered automobiles two to one. Most of the black men here worked for the white landowners or with the sawmills or other low paying jobs and spendable income was low. A free barbecue as a condition of listening to a politician wasn't a bad way to spend Sunday afternoon to most people here. Several white and black men served behind makeshift tables, dishing up good-smelling food to the long line of hungry people. We got in the rear of the line and waited our turn for the paper plate full of good-smelling meat, pork and beans, potato salad, and sliced bread. Big paper cups of half-cold tea were handed to us at the end of the table along with a toothy man smiling and saying. "Now y'all remember who to vote for, come primary time."

The choir was into its third hymn when a cloud of dust could be seen coming down the road from the east. Four big cars sped into the driveway of the church. The lead car and the last car had Georgia State Patrol insignia on the doors. As the dust settled, the gray-clad troopers in the lead car exited and quickly walked to the second car. One of them opened the door and out came the tall governor. He vigorously walked to the raised platform the choir was on and held his arms outstretched for silence.

"Folks, we are at a crossroads in the state of Georgia. I'm for going straight through the crossroads. I'm also for putting more of the state's money into Negro schools and colleges. I would like to see a minimum wage standard across the whole state of twenty five cents an hour. I would spend more time with you today but the good folks at the church in the next community are waiting. Thank you and remember who to vote for come primary time. After I win the Democratic primary, I'm going to have a Republican to face in November so vote then too. I hope you enjoyed the barbecue."

He started back to his car with four state troopers around him. When he walked past the spot where the five of us sat on the grass Wash called, "Governor, can I ask you for a favor?"

The big man stopped not more than a few feet away from us and looked down at the now standing Wash. He knelt so that he would be at eye level with my friend and said. "Son, even though you can't vote, you can ask me anything you want."

Wash cleared his throat and said. "Me and Luke and Becky are the best friends in the world." He turned and indicated who me and Becky were. "Luke's grandpa shot and killed Reuben Squire because he married Beth who is his daughter and Luke's aunt and Reuben wouldn't quit beating Beth up. Alex is gonna go to the electric chair if you don't pardon him. Me and Luke and Becky will vote for you when we get older if you'll pardon him now."

The governor said, "Young man, if your friend's grandpa don't get off before I go out of office, the three of you come to see me and I'll give this case my undivided attention, and if it is as you say, then I will pardon Luke's grandpa."

"Are you sure you'll remember us?"

He called the photographer accompanying the entourage over to where we were and said, "Sam, take a picture of me and these children with the black choir in the background. Release the picture to all the major newspapers in the state this week." He left without answering Wash.

We rode home slower than we came. Obviously all the women had been spoken for, because Chilie didn't say much. When he let Lucy and Queen out he drove to the street two blocks from Becky's house and let her out. When we were driving into our drive he looked into the rearview mirror at me and asked, "Luke, do you think they is going to send Mr. Alex to the electric chair?"

"You heard the governor just like I did. He said he would give this case his undivided attention."

"I've went to that same church for years, and I've ate this man's barbecue and a half-dozen other politicians' barbecue. I've listened to them all say the same things over and over. Ain't nothing changed in the last forty years. He's just saying things to get folks to vote for him."

This made me sad.

Pete was home. Wash's mother was in his car waiting. She wasn't sitting on the far right side. More to the middle. When we drove up Pete came out of the front door and waved. "Hello, boys. We brought you a surprise back from the wedding. Where's Becky? We brought her one too."

I had never seen Pete this happy. Wash wasn't happy though. At least he didn't look very happy.

Pete drove Wash and Mrs. Jackson home, and I went inside, half expecting my mother to question me about why I still had on my Sunday clothes. I don't even think she saw me. She was sitting in an overstuffed chair with a wet hand towel folded across her head, which was as far back on the back rest of the chair as possible.

"What's the matter, Mother?"

"Your grandfathers are going to be the death of me yet. Your grandfather Pete is trying to act like a young Romeo now. After all the problems Alex's having I wish he would act his age."

I went upstairs and changed clothes.

Cotton was ripe enough and opened enough to harvest, so for the next several weeks me and Wash rode with Chilie or Alex to the fields.

Occasionally Pete would come out late in the afternoons and help with the weighing. Becky would come with us when she was sure that her mother wouldn't find out. Twice in August Mrs. Taylor took Saturday afternoon off and the same days Alex took special interest in his personal hygiene and left in the car by himself. No explanation offered.

Since I was a small child I thought that each new season offered more pleasing sensations than the last. The smells of trees and flowers changed from month to month and offered a cornucopia of sensations that pleased my eyes and nose and mind. The smells of dog days were uncommonly good this year. Plants ripening their fruits and seeds that would ensure their continued lineage particularly pleased my senses and the cotton and peanuts in the fields and the trees and shrubs of the roadsides and forests mixed their wild smells with the smells of man grown plants. Life was good, except for the approaching day on a calendar in September that all the wishing in the world wouldn't prevent from getting here, nor all the money in the world keep the sun from coming up each morning and another day going by, getting closer to that day in September.

Three days before school started Frankie Robin knocked the chain gang guard in the head with a shovel and he and twenty-three other convicts escaped. A half-dozen short-timers waited patiently in the prison bus with their feet shackled to the seats until someone from the county work camp came looking for them. The escaped prisoners walked into the dense Pachitla Creek Swamp, where they had been cleaning the road shoulders, and disappeared. Frankie took the guard's shotgun and pistol.

According to who you were talking to, Frankie was the meanest boy ever raised in our town. I had been around him many times though and he didn't seem that mean to me. His eyes always smiled as if to say, "I'm going to do this mean thing because it will be funny to me and because I don't give a damn what you think." His widowed mother had tried to raise him by herself and through no fault of her own had raised a very bad boy. Before he was ten years old he stayed in trouble, causing his mother embarrassment and pain. The law in town ineffectively tried to make a law abider out of him. The ministers and school teachers failed miserably to break his mean spirit.

Behind his mother's house was an ill-tended vegetable garden that abutted the back of Mrs. Lunsford's well-tended garden. Mrs. Lunsford's house fronted on the next street that ran parallel and behind Mrs. Robin's house. The tall, lanky, slightly retarded Lunsford boy was painting the back of his mother's house, high on a ladder, when Frankie thought it would be funny if he shot the Lunsford boy off the ladder with a small-caliber rifle. The boy didn't die, but he never got on a ladder again and Frankie went to jail. Now he was out with the guard's rifle and pistol and presumably in Pachitla swamp.

The excitement over the next few days had a tendency to dilute the feeling of impending doom that had settled over our house. As Pete said on several occasions, "Has anyone noticed Chilie's not spouting any smart-assed answers lately? I wonder what's wrong with him."

Bloodhounds were brought in from the work camps located in several of the counties around our county. The affair turned into a virtual sideshow when one of the farmers south of town found a note stuck in his back door that had been left some time in the late hours the night before. "I'm going to kill every man in Chickasaw and rape every woman. I'm going to cook and eat every young 'un. Signed— Frankie Robin."

When me and Wash met Becky at the bandstand and walked to Mr. Weldon's the town was full of people and every man walking the streets had a pistol strapped to his waist and a shotgun in his hands. Mr. Weldon grumbled to us that the fools with the guns were hurting his trade. "Why in the name of hell don't they go to the swamp to look for Frankie? The boy's not in town. Those fools are going to wind up drunk and by night everybody they see is going to look like Frankie. If y'all come to town after five, I'm not going to be here."

"I'll ask Chilie if he'll drive you home at five o'clock, Mr. Weldon," I volunteered.

"Well, thank you, Luke, that would be mighty nice. When y'all leave here will you take Mrs. Robin's prescription by her house. Poor old soul. She's been on the verge of a nervous breakdown for the last few days. This isn't anything but sweetened whiskey but it'll do her good."

When Wash knocked on Mrs. Robin's door the aroma of fresh-baked cookies seeped from the cracks around the door of her house. After several minutes of knocking and calling, we didn't get any response.

I told them, "Mrs. Robin is as deaf as a post. See if the door will open." It did and we followed the smell of good cookies baking down the hall. The three of us walked through the dark hall toward the back of the house. I could hear the bustling of someone busy in the kitchen and smell the unknown but delicious aromas that had met us at the front door. When we walked into the kitchen a clean shaven and neat man sat at the kitchen table eating. Sharp blue eyes that seemed to be laughing looked at the three of us almost disinterestedly. Frankie Robin was calmly eating dinner in newly washed and ironed clothes as if no more had happened than him dropping by for a casual visit with his mother. She was happy beyond words that her Frankie was home. She didn't believe that he deserved the treatment he had received from the hands of the authorities.

I managed to blurt, "Mr. Weldon asked us to bring your medicine by your house. Didn't nobody hear us knocking. I'm sorry we busted in on you, Mrs. Robin."

Frankie looked hard, then a telltale sign appeared that indicated he had recognized one or all of us, and a smile punctuated his face. "Hello. You're the Campbell boy, aren't you? And this handsome boy and pretty girl must be, wait don't tell me, the beautiful women who work at the laundry. You're their children." He smiled broadly as if genuinely pleased that he had guessed right.

The three of us stood speechless and wide-eyed. Was this the notorious criminal that the whole town had armed itself against? "You're Frankie Robin?" Becky uttered, more statement than question.

"That I be, beautiful lady, and what is your name?"

"Becky. Becky Taylor. And this is Wash and Luke."

"Pleased to meet you gentlemen. Mama, do you think you could check those cookies in the oven? These folks look like they could use a big ole peanut butter cookie."

I figured that if he was going to kill us we might as well die with our bellies full of peanut butter cookies, so we sat at the table and the most sought after criminal in the state of Georgia poured us a glass of iced tea and placed two big cookies on a small plate in front of each of us. We ate and listened to the man and I totally enjoyed every minute of it.

"Y'all are going to be famous," he told us. "You can make up all the lies you want to about me. You can tell all your friends that I held a pistol on you and made you eat my mother's cookies." He laughed and the three of us got tickled and couldn't stop laughing.

Mrs. Robin said in a firm voice, "I don't cook that bad."

Becky told her, "No, ma'am, these are the best cookies I ever ate." Mrs. Robin smiled.

Wash said, "Anytime you get a notion to cook any cookies, Mrs. Robin, me and my friends would sure like to visit you."

After we had finished our cookies and tea, Frankie said, and his eyes weren't laughing this time, "Would you three do me a big favor? It'll make you sure enough famous. I need somebody to stay here with my mother while I go and borrow a car. You can tell all your friends that I kidnapped you."

Wash looked at Frankie suspiciously and asked, "Are you going to shoot us like you did Jamie Lunsford if we don't?"

"Wash, that was a mistake. I didn't mean to shoot Lunsford. I've needed glasses since I was a little child, but I argued with my mother that I wouldn't wear them. I really am sorry, but you should have seen that lanky son of a bitch falling down the ladder." All of us laughed at the mental image he evoked.

When he got back to the house, he was driving the only police car that Chickasaw owned. Someone had left a policeman's hat in the back seat, and Frankie had it on. He came into the house, leaving the front door open and the engine running in the police car. "Well, Mama, I guess I'd best be going. I enjoyed visiting with you and the dinner was delicious." He hugged her and turned toward us. We knew that we didn't have a choice, so we went with a smile on our faces. Everyone wanted to sit in the front seat, so Frankie finally decided that we could all squeeze in.

We waved to everyone we saw. When Frankie got to the bridge that spanned Little Pachitla creek north of town, he stopped the car and said, "I'm sorry that you have to walk home but I can't take you back. I want you to act like I kidnapped you so that you won't get in trouble." He shook hands with us before he left. "Tell Mama I'll see her Thanksgiving. Why don't you guys come around that afternoon? I'll make sure Mama has some more cookies." He was gone in a cloud of dust, and I felt extremely sad.

"Why don't we ask the governor to excuse him when he excuses Alex?" Wash asked.

"I hope he gets away," Becky said to no one.

"Me too."

"Me three."

Chapter Twelve

MAYOR CARLTON GOT RIP-ROARING DRUNK. The two-man police force was the shame of the town and subsequently the shame of the mayor because he was responsible for them. Alex and Pete laughed harder than I had ever seen either of them do when Chilie told us about the police in Atlanta finding the car in a parking lot downtown with a note from Frankie telling Mayor Carlton that he appreciated the use of the police car. Now the mayor was drunk and seeking revenge.

Sister Ruby called Alex. She was on the verge of becoming hysterical. "Alex, get downtown, quick! Carlton is standing in the middle of the street waving a pistol and shouting for poor Mr. Carstell to come out of the police station with his hands up."

"Hold on, Ruby. Slow down. Why's Carlton threatening his policeman?"

"Mr. Carstell was on duty when Frankie stole the car. Carlton's mad because everybody in the county is laughing about it."

I wasn't going to miss this for anything. I didn't ask anyone's permission to go. I walked out with Alex and got in the back seat. When we got to town the mayor had shot a hole in the window of the little room where the police had an office. He had Mr. Carstell on the sidewalk sitting in a straight chair. When we stopped he told Mr. Carstell in a loud and stern voice. "Do it again. Let's see what Alex thinks."

"Please, Mr. Carlton, I don't want to do it again."

Carlton pointed his pistol and Mr. Carstell stuck his hands out in front as if he were grasping a steering wheel and pursed his mouth into an O and said, "Waaaaaaaaawaaaaaaaawaaaah."

"Goddammit, Carstell, you still don't sound like a siren."

"What're you doing, Carlton?" Alex asked as we got out of the car.

"We ain't got no police car so I'm making the one what let it get stole act like a police car. Louder, Carstell."

"Give me the pistol before you hurt somebody," Alex told him.

Tears began running down the big mayor's cheeks. "Everybody's laughing about this, Alex."

Alex put his arm around the big man's shoulder and said, "Booty, stop and think about it. It wasn't your fault or Carstell's fault that the police car got stolen. There was enough men and guns in this little town to have changed the outcome of the War between the States if it had taken place back then. Just think about it, man. Frankie comes home and eats a good meal then walks downtown in broad daylight and gets our only police car. I think it's the funniest thing that's ever happened here."

They stood there side by side for a full minute staring at the white brick wall of the police and fire station. All at once the mayor made a strange "whoop" sound. He and Alex whooped and slapped their knees and finally sat flat down and whooped and hollered and laughed until they held their sides in pain. Everyone around had joined in and was laughing. Sister Ruby was glued to the front window of her upstairs telephone exchange. She called several people, including my mother, and told them that the grown men in the street had all lost all reasoning powers but there wasn't anyone to call for help. She said that all the people that she had once considered sane were down there in the street rolling around and laughing. We drove Mayor Carlton home, and Alex told him he would see him tomorrow and bring his gun back to him. On the way to the mayor's house Alex and Mr. Carlton had several drinks from a quart bottle of liquor, and the mayor cried and told Alex he would go to the electric chair for him.

"I pay my own debts, Booty."

"But hell's bells, Alex, I ain't got a soul on earth but my wife and dog and don't neither one of them like me. You got Luke here and Beth and Clementine to see about. I'm going to speak to Judge Greer if he's sober tomorrow morning to see if I can take your place."

"Don't worry, Booty. They haven't decided what to do with me yet."

"Well, I'm going to ask the city council to vote to give you a reward for getting rid of a pestilence."

Alex and I drove home in silence. The hearing was two weeks away.

School started, and me and Becky and Wash still stayed away from the others when we had recess and lunch break.

The first few days people looked at us curiously as if wondering how we could still be friends after all that had happened that summer. After the first week no one bothered us at all. Most of the farm kids hadn't come back to school yet. This was harvest time and they would take most of the allowable absences before they came back. I supposed that one by one me and Becky would be subjected to their curious stares at some later date.

Sheriff Gaines came by our house and told Alex that he would come get him the following week on the day of the hearing.

"You don't need to come get me. I'll be there. I'll ride over with Pete. I'll need to talk to him about a few things."

"I'm going too," I told them.

Alex said, "You can ride with your mother and Lucy. Chilie will drive."

For the first time in my life I squared my jaw against my grandfather. "No, sir. They can ride by themselves. I'm riding with you and Pete."

He looked at me in a funny way. Not mad at me and not overly surprised at me standing up to him. He looked back at the sheriff and said, "As I was saying I'll ride over with Pete and Luke if that's all right."

"That suits me fine, Alex. Just be there by 9:45. Court starts at ten, and I imagine that Judge Greer has you scheduled first."

"I'll be there."

"Alex he's going to ask you how you plead. For God's sake, man, just tell him you want to plead guilty to manslaughter."

"See you next week, Sheriff."

Time, from that moment until the next week, seemed to be encapsulated in some strange substance that one could almost feel. I looked at things in strange ways because they seemed alien to my senses. Everything seemed to happen in slow motion, but the days were passing at a frightening speed. I slept fitfully and dreamed of my father's funeral that Monday night, and when I awoke, I knew that this would be a very important day.

Alex tried to act cheerful at breakfast, but every few seconds he would look at his gold railroad watch and say, "I guess we had best leave. We may have a flat and I don't want the judge to fine me for being late. You never can tell, the man might send me to jail. I'm going to check on Beth, then we'll leave."

At nine I got in the front seat between Alex and Pete in Pete's car. My mother and Lucy, both wearing the best that they owned, got in the back seat of Alex's car and Chilie almost ceremoniously cranked the big car. Alex had told him before we left, "Chilie, you cut one fine figure of a man dressed up the way you are. I'll bet all the single black women in town seek your company."

"I'd give 'em all up, Mr. Alex, if you'd come home with us this evening."

When we got to the city limits of Trinity, I knew that something big and very unusual was happening. Cars, buggies with one horse, wagons with two mules, old pickup trucks, even two church buses, were lining the road on each side leading to the square. About a quarter mile from the town square we saw them. Hundreds and hundreds of people. People dressed in their best, farmers in overalls, schoolchildren, old people, young people. When we slowly drove past, all the men took their hats off and the women and children held their hands up and to a person they had their fingers crossed as if to say, "We hope for you, we wish for you." When we reached the square the crowds were thicker. No one smiled as they watched us turn slowly toward the courthouse. A few men shouted, "Good luck, Alex." A few women said, "We're praying for you, Alex." My eyes felt funny and Alex and Pete kept swallowing loudly and blinking fast. Alex pulled his handkerchief out and blew his nose loudly. Pete did the same. Neither man could look at the other.

Sheriff Gaines looked as solemn as an undertaker when Pete stopped his car in front of the courthouse. He had secretly hoped that Alex would just leave and never be heard from again. "Why is something like this happening in an election year?" he asked anyone willing to hear.

The courtroom was packed. The balcony was full and the halls and stairs were full of orderly people wishing their best and hoping things turned out well. Most of them held up their right hands with their first and second fingers crossed.

Judge Greer walked through the back door at exactly ten o'clock and Sheriff Gaines jumped to his feet and screamed, "Atten-shun! I'm sorry, Judge, I was in the army. All rise."

When the formalities were over and all the accused were accounted for, the district attorney signaled the sheriff and he faced the people and said, "The state calls the first case, one Luther Alex Campbell, accused of murder in the first degree. The defendant will approach the bench."

The judge looked down at Alex through the lower half of his thick bifocals and said, "You, Alexander Campbell, have been accused of murder in the first degree. Since this is somewhat unusual in my district I'm going to deviate from protocol and ask you a few questions before I take your plea." He cleared his throat and drank a swallow of water before continuing. "Did the man you are accused of killing try to harm you in any way?"

"No, your honor."

"Did he hint or insinuate that he might carry a lethal weapon on his person?"

"No, your honor."

"Did he curse you or say vile and blasphemous things about your person or about any member of your family?"

"No."

"What did he say? I'll ask all the women and children to cover their ears."

"Nothing. I just shot him."

"Alex, I'm fighting for your life. Were you afraid he'd pull a gun? What did you do then?"

"I shot him in bed. He was asleep."

"Seems odd to me. Him being in bed."

"I guess he was drunk."

"You leave me no escape, Alex. You have been accused of murder in the first degree. How plead you?"

"Guilty."

"Alex, you leave me no choice. The state of Georgia mandates death by the electric chair for murder." He paused for a full five minutes. He looked up at the ceiling. He looked hard at me and my mother. "I sentence you, Alex Campbell, to be put to death as the state of Georgia mandates on November thirtieth of this year. May God have mercy on you." He swallowed hard and continued, "Sheriff Gaines, I want you to go directly to your office and call the governor and ask for a general pardon. Tell him while you're at it that I'm resigning from this goddam job, so appoint somebody to take my place."

He got up from his chair and the sheriff called, "All rise."

The judge walked quickly to the door he had entered a few minutes earlier. He turned again to the sheriff before he disappeared. "I hereby declare all others that supposed to come before me today innocent by default. Turn them loose."

Five men accused of various crimes sat in the wing behind the sheriff. They looked expectant. Sheriff Gaines said, "Get the hell out of here and don't let me catch you in the county again."

We all knew what to expect when we came here, but it didn't lessen the numbness that everyone felt. No one cried, not even my mother. That would come later. Silently we all rose and followed Alex down the aisle toward the exit. Sheriff Gaines called, "Alex, I think I'm supposed to keep you." He paused then said, "Aw, to hell with it, I'll come get you when it's time."

We walked single-file out of the courthouse and the silent crowd parted before us as a diminishing wave would retreat from the shore line. Some of the men timidly reached to shake Alex's hand as he passed. No one uttered a sound. Most of the women dabbed at wet eyes for the man who stood up for women being mistreated and now had to die for it.

At supper that night Alex and Pete talked sparingly. When I didn't say anything for a long time, my mother asked, "What are you thinking, Luke? You're awfully quiet."

"I was thinking that if you want justice you go to the whorehouse."

She didn't know which of my grandfathers to get mad at so she didn't say anything.

Alex made an announcement when we finished the meal. "I've made up my mind that I'm not going to be executed for something that needed doing. I want all of you to rest well tonight because tomorrow I've got to start thinking of ways to keep me out of Reidsville."

"We all have to start thinking of ways to keep you out," Pete said.

Chapter Thirteen

ON SATURDAY ME, WASH, AND BECKY, were walking down the dirt sidewalk by the main road leading into town. The old school bus, painted white, passed us, and the driver blew his horn and waved prodigiously. On the side of the bus written in bright crimson a sign proclaimed "Evangelist Munroe P. Grimes—Healer of lost souls— Proclaimer of the faith." Big double morning-glory loudspeakers were attached to the top of the bus. As he drove slowly past, the loudspeakers came alive. "Good morning. I want to invite you to our revival. Praise the Lord. Come worship with us in the pecan grove south of town tomorrow afternoon at three o'clock. The Lord will bless you. Come let us introduce you to your, and my own, personal savior." We heard the message booming all over town.

In small towns in the South, people relied on the traveling evangelists that came to town to seek out the sinners, not of the flock, to be saved. These sinners shunned the call of the local ministers as a rule and stayed away from Sunday services but answered the siren call of the tent preachers. Most often as not the sinners often succumbed to the annual salvation just for the excitement of it. Sometimes the "saving" lasted. Most times though the temptations offered by the devil overcame with a short passing of time and put the sinner back in his fold. Strong drink and the passing of time dimmed the passing preacher's sermons. This suited the traveling ministers to a tee. When they came back to town again the same lost sheep would need saving again.

We walked straight past Mr. Weldon's, and the now eight flavors of ice cream (he had added cherry) and on to the pecan grove south of town. When we got there, three women were sitting in canvas bottomed chairs under the spreading trees. They were vigorously fanning the insects away with paper fans that depicted a facsimile of Jesus with a halo over his head on the front. Three sweating men were rolling out the carcass of a bright yellow tent that when fully erected would seat almost two hundred lost and sinful souls. Hell's fires wouldn't see many souls from Chickasaw County for the next several days.

"You want to make yourself a shiny new dime?" The older man asked us.

Not one to turn down money, Wash answered, "Doing what."

"Getting the chairs out of the back of that bus and setting them up."

"A dime each or a dime between us?"

"Is your pap a lawyer?" The man said, smiling as he asked.

"He's dead, but he always told me to bite the coin to make sure it was real." We worked hard carrying folding chairs and lining them up just so. The rows had to be curved perfectly so all the congregation could face the preacher. Each row had to be spaced far enough apart to insure that a sinner that had been called could come forth with relative ease. So many times strong drink would enhance the inner hearing of certain members of the congregation and they would hear the Lord calling and walk down that aisle. By 4:00 the tent was full of chairs, the raised platform with the big podium was in place, and the piano had been placed at the far right of the platform. Green runners, three feet wide stretched from the front entrance to the stage. The sides of the tent were rolled up and tied at the top. The oldest of the three men checked everything under the tent. He tested each key on the piano, he shook the tent poles, he walked from the front of the tent to the back slowly and looked at each row of chairs, then he walked up the green runner to the small raised platform and adjusted the speakers podium until it was perfect. This would be the place where he pounded his fist and thundered his loud voice across the heads of those lost sheep. New crop cotton money was in the hands of so many that would come through those yellow flaps and he intended to get his and the Lord's share. He would do the dividing.

"I couldn't interest you three into sharing this dime with the Lord, could I?" he asked as he reluctantly handed us each a dime.

Becky told him, "I didn't see the Lord helping us tote chairs. I want all of mine."

"Then could I employ the three of you to pass the offering plate each time we have service?"

"What do we have to do and how much does it pay?" She asked him.

He nodded in the direction of a buxom woman wearing heavy makeup. Her blonde hair was piled high on her head.

I suspected that at some earlier time in life she had been quite pretty. "When Miss Lily starts playing "Just As I Am" on the piano, the three of you will start at the front of the church, one in the middle and the other two on the outside of the seats. The reason we start at the front is because the folks on the front rows know that the folks behind them are watching to see how much they give and they'll give more to the Lord. The two on the outside start the collection plates and when the plate gets to the middle aisle the one in the middle gives it to the next row."

"How much?"

"The Lord said in the book of Matthew that 'Ye can not serve two masters, Ye cannot serve God and Mammon.' Mammon being money. Young lady, it seems that you have chosen to serve mammon."

"How much?"

"Ten cents apiece each service, fifteen cents on the last night."

"Mister, at a nickel an hour you've already beat us out of fifteen cents. We'll do it for twenty cents each night and fifty cents the last night."

"The Lord said in the book of Ephesians. 'Those, because of the blindness of their heart: who being past feelings have given themselves over to lasciviousness, to work all uncleanliness with greediness.' The Lord don't look kindly on greediness, young lady."

"Mister, you know that if us little kids pass the plate, people will give more. We want our money in advance each night."

We got the job and a ten-minute sermon concerning greed.

At some point in the sermon each night the preacher or one of the assistants would lapse into a spate of speaking in an unknown tongue. Each time this was explained as the Lord taking control of the mortal's voice box and speaking as the people of Babel. It sounded like gibberish to me, but by midweek numerous people in the congregation had fallen out in the middle of the aisle and started speaking in the unknown tongue.

Lum Chestnut was dead drunk when he got the spirit. He rolled in the aisle yelling gibberish, his eyes rolling in his head, and his body arched in contortions and spasms. The preacher had spent the past few minutes of the sermon bashing the vices of conspicuous consumption. Throwing one's money away on the vanities or the vices was next to heresy. All spare money should go to the ministries, according to the preacher. When Lum refocused his blurred vision he pulled a pint of white whiskey from his right pocket and threw it out of the tent then he took his unopened can of Prince Albert tobacco out of his other pocket and threw it out the other side of the tent. By the time the service was over he had regained enough of the frailties of human nature to suffer from tobacco withdrawal and a mild case of D.T.'s simultaneously. When we left the tent that night, after having helped straighten the chairs and pick up the litter, Lum was crawling on his hands and knees looking for his far flung belongings. He had unwittingly given away all his money to the collection plate and this was going to be a long week for him.

Miss Lily played the piano and the two men and two ladies sang. The congregation was instructed when to join the singing, usually on a chorus line. The opening hymn and the closing hymn were sung in their entirety by the entire congregation. The invitational hymn was a solo by one of the tired-looking women.

Friday, the last night of tent revival, Wash stole five dollars out of the collection plate. When I asked him on Saturday where he got the money he said, "That man stole all week and we helped. I didn't think the Lord would think any less of me for keeping the money in the community."

He made sense.

We walked past the trampled spot where the big tent had been all week that Saturday afternoon and Lum Chestnut was walking around in the tall grass still looking for his belongings. We stopped and asked if we could help. "I'd be much obliged."

"Why did you throw your liquor and tobacco away?" Wash asked him.

"I'm damned if I know, must of been a lapse of sanity like I had that time in Ragsdale."

"What's Ragsdale?" I asked the man.

"You mean Alex ain't told you about Ragsdale yet?"

"No sir."

"Well, if somebody offers to take you to Ragsdale don't go."

"What is it?" I asked again.

"Up in Albany, down by the river, there's a line of old two-story houses they turned into whorehouses. Thirteen or fourteen of them. I rode over there with Charlie one time before he wrecked his car. I paid some woman three dollars for some you know what. Regretted it ever since. Most overrated thing I ever heard of."

There was that "you know what" again.

We looked where the seats had been. I found several pennies and a nickel. Becky found a fifty-cent piece. Lum didn't find what he was looking for.

School was vile, it was something that should be taken out and shot at dawn. I didn't see any reason for me to go. I was as smart as I needed to be and once you knew the three R's I didn't see the point in going any longer. September carried a new emphasis for me now that I knew Alex was going to die. This would be his very last Indian summer. The days when the dog star was closest to the earth had come and gone before Alex's hearing. Harsh then, the weather was now mellow and easy. I wondered what Alex thought of when he and I walked through the trees and watched the squirrels gathering autumn's fruit and making plans for the coming spring. "Are you scared?" I asked him one September morning when the sky was uncommonly blue.

"No. Yes. I don't have … I don't want to die and not see you become a man. I think this. I think that you are going to be a good man and a man of greatness, of magnificence, and I don't want to miss that."

"If you think that, then I'm going to get permission for you to wait until I grow up before you have to die."

He smiled the saddest smile I've ever seen.

Sister Ruby told me the next week that when the cock crowed at sundown someone you loved was going to die. I avoided the chicken yard for fear I would hear the cock.

Pete asked Mrs. Jackson to marry him, and she said no. I found out from Wash. She had a logical explanation. She told

Pete that she couldn't think about anything until she had gotten Mrs. Taylor through the bad times she was going through and they would all go through this November. Pete was visibly hurt and wouldn't speak cordially to anyone. He brightened up considerably the next week when he and Mr. O. Z. planned a fishing trip to the saltwater flats on the coast southwest of Tallahassee, Florida. He told me. "The speckled trout are biting, according to one of O. Z.'s cousins who lives down there. I'll be back in a week or two, maybe sooner. I don't know how long I can tolerate O. Z. at one spell."

"Why don't you take me with you? It would give you somebody to talk to when you got mad with him like you always do."

"Have you skipped any days from school yet?"

"No sir. Your daughter teaches in the class room next to mine, and she won't give me an excuse."

"I'll ask her tonight at dinner."

We sat down to a delicious meal that night and many compliments and praises were bestowed on my mother. A good conversation flowed around the table until Pete decided it was time to ask. "Clemmy, I would appreciate it if you would let Luke skip school for a few days to go to Florida with me and O. Z."

I could have fainted, and Pete was totally unprepared for her answer. "All right. I suppose it would do him good."

Pete must not have believed what he heard. He continued. "Clemmy, I know you don't approve of him skipping school but I think it would do the boy a world of good and I could sure use the company."

I tugged on Pete's sleeve. "She said I could go."

"Huh. By God she did, didn't she? I thought I heard that. You feel okay, Clemmy?"

"What are you going to Florida for?" Alex asked.

"O. Z. has a first cousin, some old lady who owns a hotel right on the banks of the Steinhatchee River. She wrote him last week and said he ought to come down visiting. I assume she's just a lonely old widow who misses her family. Anyways, to make a short story long, she said in her letter that the fish were biting and for him to come down if he felt so inclined. O. Z. told me the last time he saw her she was one fine-looking woman. Of course now we're talking about a man who thinks that he is the town's sex symbol."

"Would do us all good to get away for a while," Alex said.

"If you're caught up with your cotton crop enough for Chilie to tend to it why don't you come with us too."

"That's mighty nice of you to ask." He chuckled. "This might be the last crop I harvest so I guess Chilie can get it harvested without me."

I think the excitement of getting away from the pressure that we all felt must have been almost intoxicating. Alex and Pete were in better moods than I could remember in recent months and I felt like I was king for a day. Wash begged and begged the next day when he found out I was going. He pleaded with Pete to let him go too, then when he obtained Pete's permission he pleaded with his mother until she said yes. Pete had told him that he had to make it all right with everyone concerned, so he pleaded with O. Z. and Alex until he had unanimous consent. Pete told me not to tell anyone else we were going or he would have to rent a bus.

Mrs. Jackson washed and darned for Wash on Friday night, Alex spent most of the night sitting by Beth's bed, and Saturday morning, two hours before the sun even thought about coming up, we were on our way, zipping along at forty miles an hour toward the Florida line.

"Why do old people like to leave before daylight?" Wash whispered to me.

"I think that it's because the closer you get to dying the less time you want to spend asleep."

We drove in Alex's big car with him and Pete in the front and me and Wash and Mr. O. Z. in the back. Within minutes the back seat was snoring loudly. The sun was up when I awoke. Mr. O. Z. sounded like a sawmill with the jitters. The day was going to be hot. When I let the window down to get fresh air, Wash and Mr. Dean woke up. "Pull over, Alex," shouted Mr. O. Z. "My eyeballs are floating, I've got to pee so bad."

Mother had packed us a big Thermos of steaming coffee and a bag of homemade doughnuts when we left that morning. Alex pulled over, and while Mr. O. Z. relieved himself Pete poured us all a paper cup full of coffee and passed the doughnuts around. Mr. O. Z. took a long time. "Save me some of that coffee, you young whippersnappers."

"What's that thing you called us, Mr. Dean?" Wash asked.

"Well in my case it means anybody who can pee in less than five minutes."

"Why does it take you so long?" I wanted to know.

"The delivery system breaks down, Luke. When I was younger, I had enough pressure to make a crapper foam over."

"I can pee over this car," Wash stated as a matter of fact.

"I can't pee much over a foot," Mr. Dean said sadly.

"You all can change the conversation," Pete told us.

The northern portion of the state of Florida was boring and ugly as far as I was concerned. The big oaks and pines that grew so tall and prolific where we lived was suddenly replaced with bluejack oak and scrubby sand pine. The infertile white sand splashed on this part of the world wouldn't support any tree of any speakable statue. Cabbage palm and sand cactus filled the understory under the stunted full growth. Brackish water stagnated in the ditches on either side of the road and conjured up images of alligators lurking under the lily pads that dotted the black water like green periods. White egrets and blue herons strutted with their long legs and waited for unsuspecting frogs or slow minnows. I saw the first orange tree. Wash lied and said he saw a coconut tree full of coconuts and two alligators under it.

The men decided that it would be bad manners for us to show up at noon so we ate lunch at a clapboard-sided oyster shack a few miles from Mr. O. Z.'s first cousin's hotel. I ate smoked mullet and boiled shrimp. Everyone else ate raw oysters.

While we were eating, Mr. O. Z. told us what to expect when we met his cousin. "Her daddy left Georgia when the boll weevil got here. He moved to Alabama and opened a blacksmith shop. When she was born he thought that it would help business if he named her Bama Jo, so that's what he named her. She married a man from Florida who drove a Rolls-Royce back in thirty one or thirty two. Wasn't any more than sixteen at the time, she wasn't."

Pete said, "I thought she was an old woman O. Z. She's in her thirties."

"Thirty-four," Wash said.

When we reached the ocean, I asked Pete to stop the car. Me and Wash had never seen anything like that. I thought of Chilie when he drove Alex to New Orleans and he said that everywhere they drove there was just more land.

We bought gas in the small fishing village and Pete asked directions to the Dorcus Hotel. Mr. Dean had explained that Bama Jo had named the hotel after her mother and her mother had been named for her maternal grandfather who had been in line to be the Earl of Dorcus, that is, until the future Earl's wife ran off with some man from France and the earl left for America only to die destitute after a long battle with a failed liver due to excessive spirituous libation.

Massive white brick columns fronted the gravel road and supported heavy iron gates on either end of the long circular drive. On top of the square brick columns stone eagles looked down menacingly as if threatening the incoming traffic.

Hibiscus, mandivilla, date trees, and lemon, lime, orange, and grapefruit trees separated the quarter-mile between gates. In a slightly arced pattern, iron fencing connected the gates. We passed the first gate and stopped about halfway between it and the second one. A tremendous structure that resembled a plantation home aligned perfectly with the center of the fence. Acres of green grass separated the road from the hotel. In the background I could see the tannic acid stained river. The setting was beautiful and soul mending.

Mr. O. Z. had never been here but he kept saying, "See, I told you so. By golly, that's my kin."

Flowers of every color lined the curved driveway to the front of the hotel. Six massive columns, fluted from bottom to top and crowned with Georgian capitols spanned the wide porch. Big white rocking chairs with cane backs and bottoms were spaced across the length of the porch. Green ferns in large gray stone urns stood guard on either side of the double entry doors. I could imagine the late afternoons on this wide porch when waiters would bring mint juleps and cigars to rich men in white suits and string ties, and bring white wine disguised as lemonade to the ladies.

Eager to get out of the car, we all walked up the steps behind Mr. O. Z. and waited as he knocked on the door. Alex said, "Why are you knocking on the door? This is a hotel."

"I don't know, Alex. The place looks like you need to knock on the door in order to be polite."

Nobody questioned his logic, so we stood as Mr. Dean knocked for several minutes. A big woman wearing an apron came to the door and we wordlessly followed her to the tiny cubicle in the hall that advertised its function as being the office and guest registration. The big woman pushed back loose strands of hair and pointed to a palm bell. She looked at us as if to insinuate how ignorant we were then she slammed her hand down on the bell and walked back in the direction of the kitchen. A door opened down the hall, and a woman in her thirties, one of the prettiest women I had ever seen, bustled out smiling to greet us. Light brown hair with sun blond streaks was piled on top of her head. Deep blue eyes framed by long lashes looked at us as if she were truly interested in who we were. She wore a floor-length skirt that moved when she walked like graceful wild things were under the cloth, trying to break the bonds of the cloth. A soft white blouse, low-cut and long-sleeved, kept a full compliment of feminine parts in check. I looked at Pete and Alex and I do believe that if someone had slapped them on the back their eyes would have popped right out. I have never seen two men jerk their hats off as fast as they did.

Mr. Dean said, "Is that you, Bama Jo?"

She stopped and looked hard at him and said, "Cousin Zeke?"

"That's me, girl. Never did expect me to come see you, did you?"

A smile that showed that she really was glad to see him appeared, and she ran the rest of the way and hugged the old man then pushed away gently so that she could look at him. "You're just as handsome as ever, Cousin Zeke."

He looked back at us and grinned. "You sure did grow up to be a fine looking woman. Last time I saw you, you were thin as a rail."

Alex and Pete were fidgeting so I thought I had better do something. I walked up and stuck my hand out and said, "I'm Luke Campbell. I'm a friend of Mr. Dean's."

She knelt down and touched me and said, "Well I don't think I have ever seen a young man as good-looking as you are. I'm Bama Jo, and I wish you would grow up to be a grown man real quick." I fell in love instantly.

She shook hands with Alex and Pete as a man would and looked them straight in the eye. They both blushed and I think felt a little intimidated. Finally she stooped and kissed Wash on the cheek and he was in love.

For several hours that afternoon she stayed with us, and we listened as she told how she and her husband had built this massive house on the banks of the pristine river as a getaway, how she had turned the house into a twenty-room hotel when his children by a previous marriage had challenged his will and this was all she got, and how those same children had thrown away every last cent they had and were now trying to get this property.

Mr. O. Z. filled her in on his life. He told her all about us, his closest friends. The four of us frequently interrupted to properly embellish something he would be telling. The one thing he didn't mention was Alex's date with the executioner in November. Wash blurted that out.

"How did you young men get out of school to come here for a week?" She asked us this when we sat on the front porch later that afternoon.

Wash said, "My mama said I could come be with Luke when he came down here with his grandpas 'cause he won't never be able to go with both of them again."

"Oh. I don't understand."

"Mr. Alex is going to die in November."

"Now I really don't understand."

"She doesn't want to hear about that, Wash," Mr. O. Z. said.

She looked at Alex tenderly and straight in the eye and said, "Yes, I do. Do you mind, Alex?"

He shook his head so she turned to Wash and said, "Ok, tell me."

"Becky Taylor is mine and Luke's best friend in the whole world and her daddy wouldn't quit beating her and her mama up. Alex had him sent to prison for twenty years. Then Reuben, who was Alex's son in law, beat up Beth who is Alex's daughter and Luke's aunt. Alex shot him like a dog with rabies and the judge told him he had to go to the electric chair in November."

Tears were making silent lines down her cheeks when she went to Alex's chair and hugged him. "You poor brave man."

The men reached a settlement with Bama Jo. She didn't want us to pay anything for our rooms and meals but we compromised and paid full price for two rooms on the second floor and we paid for breakfast and dinner for a week. Lunch was on our own. That week we spent was the most enjoyable time I ever had. We argued and bartered and finally traded with a crusty old man who owned a fishing boat that could accommodate us all. He dispensed advice and conversation sparingly. He covered things, not to do, only once, and I learned after the first day to listen when he talked.

"The first thing to remember," Cap'n Joe told us on the trip out to the flats, "is never treat these saltwater fish like you would the fish you're used to. Don't stick your finger in their mouth to get the hook out."

Mr. O. Z. caught a bluefish about the size of my arm on his second cast. He stuck his thumb in the fish's mouth to extract the hook and the fish did what the species had been doing for several million years. When Mr. O. Z. got his bloody thumb out of the fish's mouth, he made sure he heard everything Cap'n Joe uttered from that point on. We had close to fifty pounds of fish when we docked behind the hotel late that day. Bama Jo ran down to meet us, then ran back to get the first aid kit to dress Zeke's hand. The hotel had twenty-two guests besides the five of us. She offered to buy our fish to offer on the menu that night. After much arguing, the men finally agreed to accept a day's lodging for the fish. They would have gladly given her the fish, but she insisted.

That night after supper the front porch filled with people rocking and talking amicably. Some smoked cigars, but no one drank a mint julep. A baby grand piano filled a front corner of the entrance hall and a guitar stood guard in the corner behind the piano. Bama Jo walked by and touched the keys. The big German woman who worked in the kitchen offered coffee to the guests.

"Who knows how to play a piano or a guitar? We can all join in singing," Bama Jo asked the group.

Mr. O. Z. piped up, "Alex here used to tickle the keys in his younger years. He could sure set toes to tapping."

I didn't know that Alex could play a piano. After Wash and I gave up begging him, Bama Jo asked once and he sat down on the piano stool and his fingers remembered things that his mind had forgotten. Pete, encouraged by Alex's brazen act, picked up the fat guitar, and within minutes they had toes tapping and hands clapping. It was a complete surprise to me. I had no idea either of them could play anything. Bama Jo sang solos. We all joined in singing someone's special request, and at 9:30, the hotel's hour for silence, everyone wanted Bama Jo to extend the deadline.

The next day Mr. O. Z. found a saxophone in the used appliance store in the tiny town, and that night the piano was moved to the front porch. By bedtime that night we almost had a following. People had walked from the surrounding area and sat on the lawn and joined in clapping or singing. Mr. O. Z. would step to the front and take absolute command with his horn's song and the crowd would cheer. Then Alex or Pete would emphasize their special talent and the crowd would cheer. Bama Jo extracted the loudest applause. Me and Wash were amazed. I never dreamed that those three old men had any musical talent.

The third night on the porch, me and Wash got tambourines and joined the band. The crowd on the lawn had swelled to several hundred. Word spreads quickly in small towns and the people had heard that Alex was going to die. That in itself added a certain urgency to what we were doing. It was a swan song, or the medicine man's last rain dance. We were playing Alex's last symphony and we didn't know to do anything more than play it. The fourth night we were there, the lawn, which should have seen nothing more exciting than croquet matches, played host to almost a thousand people. After Bama Jo had said goodnight to her guests, she hugged us all and declared, "I love each of you, I just can't decide which one I love the most."

Saturday slipped up on me far faster than I could even imagine. We were an item in the little town by then. That night Bama Jo had a loudspeaker system set up on the porch, and the crowd on the lawn almost reached the front gates. I had never had as much fun in my life as I did that week. The same was true for the other four in the group. Before we started playing that night, a skinny little man, who had obviously overcome a consuming fear of speaking in front of crowds stood and walked bravely up the steps. The muscles in his jaws squared his face nervously as he spoke in a broken voice. "I was beat, and my brothers was beat, and my ma was beat, until the day my pa died. I wish I'd a had somebody like Mr. Alex to stop my pa. Thank ye, Mr. Alex, for what ye did.

I'm goin' to pray every day for you." I had never heard a crowd of people make that much noise.

When we were packing on Sunday morning to go home, Bama Jo casually mentioned to me that she wished that she could go back with us for a few days. I told Alex, Pete, and Mr. Zeke, as he was called now, what she had said to me. Mr. Zeke found her and insisted that she visit him for as long as she wanted to stay. When we left Florida, Bama Jo sat in the front seat between Alex and Pete.

We drove into town late that afternoon. Evening church services were just over, and churchgoers were either milling around the front of the church or were walking home. We passed both churches on the way to Mr. Dean's house. At the first one I saw Mrs. Taylor staring at the front seat of our car, and at the second church I saw Mary Louise Jackson. When we passed she stamped her foot. Alex nor Pete saw either one of them, they were too busy talking to Bama Jo. That night I dreamed that our band was playing at the Grand Ole Opry and that when Alex excused himself to get killed the rest of us just kept playing.

School was worse than ever the next day. I wished that we could all go back to Florida and fish for a living. I thought that maybe when Bama Jo went back home I could go with her and live. I knew that I had all of school that I ever wanted or needed.

Chapter Fourteen

ON MONDAY AFTERNOON AFTER SCHOOL I rode my bike to Mr. O. Z.'s house to look for Bama Jo. She wasn't there, so I rode by the train depot to ask where she was. Alex's car was parked there and so was Pete's. It didn't take a genius to figure out where Bama Jo was. She was sitting on the counter where the telegraph sat and where Mr. Dean sold passenger tickets and filled out freight manifests. When she saw me, her eyes brightened and she smiled as if she was genuinely glad to see me. "Hello, partner. Was school as bad as your expression tells me it was?"

"Yep. I made up my mind that if you'll let me, I'm going back to Florida with you, and fish for a living. We could have a band and charge money to play."

She smiled. "Who would we get to play the piano or the saxophone and guitar?"

"Maybe we could hire these old geezers."

John Smith was sitting on the steps leading up to the freight room. "I can play a harmonica. Can I join your band too?"

"You can't keep from talking long enough to play a harmonica John Smith. And I'm not an old geezer, Luke smart-butt," Mr. O. Z. told him and me. To prove him wrong John Smith rose from the steps and went into the freight room. The strains of "Jimmy Crack Corn and I Don't Care" played on a harmonica perfectly, came sweetly through the partially open door.

"It appears to me that if we ever want to play again we have found a harmonica player," Pete told Mr. O. Z.

"Seems that way," Alex said.

I asked them, "Do you want to be in me and Bama Jo's band?"

"Count me in," Mr. Dean said. "I haven't had as much fun since I was a boy."

Wash popped his grinning head in the door. "Boy hydee, I know two women who are mad, and I mean mad as hornets, with Alex and Pete."

"Count me in too," Alex said.

"Me too," Pete added.

Me and Wash rode with John Smith on his dray to Mr. O. Z.'s house. Alex and Pete met us there and after many, many hells and damns, we got the piano from the front hall onto the dray. Back at the depot it was a little easier because John Smith's dray was built the same height as the loading platform. We set up in the freight room, and twenty minutes later John Smith played his first music with an all-white band.

It was after six o'clock and the train station was closed for the day, so Mr. O. Z. had locked all the doors and we were in the freight room. Two times Mr. O. Z. interrupted the playing and sent John Smith to fetch something for him. When Mr. O. Z. looked at John Smith the third time, Alex held his hands up and said, "O. Z., when John Smith is playing his harmonica with us he is a member of our group, under no obligation to wait on your lazy butt at this time. From now on, don't interrupt what we're doing or I'm leaving." Mr. O. Z. looked at everyone else and faced nods of agreement.

Bama Jo sang "Battle Hymn of the Republic" and her clear, near-perfect voice filled the dark freight room. When her sad song was over John Smith had tears running down his face. "Miss Bama Jo that's about the prettiest thing I ever heard."

Someone was beating loudly on the big wooden doors that opened onto the incoming freight platform. "Who is it?" Mr. O.Z. shouted.

"It's Robert E. Lee Carlton, that's who. Who's asking?"

"The depot's closed for the day, Carlton."

"I'm going to hook a log chain to the platform and snatch it off the building with my truck if you don't open the door, O. Z."

John Smith interceded, "Please, Mr. O. Z., open the door. I don't want to spend all the week fixing the platform."

The door was opened and the 280-pound mayor walked in and looked around. He looked hurt. "Y'all are in here having fun and you didn't invite me." He saw Bama Jo and snatched his hat off. "How do, ma'am."

"I am fine, sir." She paused as if waiting for something. "Since these gentlemen won't properly introduce us, I'm Bama Jo."

We played for about an hour, and then it was too dark in the freight room. The mayor was in love. He would have willingly left his wife and dog, given away his sawmill and farm, given up being mayor, and denounced God and the Democratic party if Bama Jo had so much as crooked her finger.

The past few days had molded the six of us into a group that was clannish but not to the point that we couldn't accept new members. We welcomed John Smith and Mayor Carlton into this select bunch but with conditions. Alex laid them down to the mayor like I suspect Moses did when he came down the mountain. First and foremost, no cussing in front of Bama Jo, second, no drinking in front of Bama Jo, no fighting in her presence, and last but most important, no flirting with Bama Jo.

The conditions were accepted by Mr. Carlton.

We sat on the depot platform that evening, and occasionally Alex or Pete would mention the fact that "Clemmy is going to be anxious about us," but no one moved. Even though it was late September and most insects had made preparations for winter, the fireflies were still signaling in the park across the street from the depot as if celebrating the first rites of spring instead of the season of the ending. The old bandstand's silhouette stood silently. Its post-sunset solitude conjured up memories for the older men of times before the war when almost every Sunday afternoon something happened in this tiny park. The town militia had built the bandstand in the 1890s and the town's drum and bugle corps had sent its finest off three times to face an enemy across the oceans. I thought that in every small town in America the finest young men had been sacrificed and died to satisfy the political ambitions and impotent chest beatings of the old men who liked war.

"We've got to come up with a plan," Bama Jo stated as fact.

"What on earth are you talking about?" O. Z. asked his cousin.

"We're living each day not daring to mention the unmentionable, watching each day go by and not doing a damned thing. We've got to stop acting as if nothing is wrong. We've got to think of some way to get Alex out of being executed. There's a way to do it if we think hard enough."

O. Z. said, "I've suggested to Alex that he go back and tell the judge that Reuben pulled a knife or something. He just tells me that he don't lie and he pays his own debts. If it was me I'd tell the judge that Reuben pulled a knife, a gun, a straight razor, and a bow and arrow on me and when they couldn't find the weapons I'd say, `well that's my story and I'm sticking to it."

Mayor Carlton said, "I think we ought to go bomb the county seat and if that don't do any good we ought to go bomb the statehouse."

Wash raised his hand as if he were in school. Everyone welcomed another suggestion even though it was coming from someone so small. "The governor told me, Becky, and Luke to come see him if the judge sentenced you to the electric chair, when he came through here back in the summer."

"The Democratic primary is over, and a Republican governor hasn't been elected since Reconstruction. He doesn't remember one in a million of his promises," Alex told us.

"Then we'd best try to polish his memory a bit," Pete suggested.

Bama Jo held her hands up and said in an excited voice, "That's it. That's the key. Did he specifically tell you that he would pardon Alex?" She looked at me and Wash.

It was my turn to talk. "He told us that if my grandpa didn't get off before he got out of office to come see him and he would give this case his undivided attention and if what we told him was true he would pardon Alex."

Carlton said, "I think I'll go beat him up if he says he don't remember."

She held up her hands again. "We've got six weeks from tomorrow until the general election. By the first Tuesday in November we had better make sure he remembers this one particular promise. Luke, can you and Wash get Becky and the three of you meet me at the laundry after school tomorrow? Pete, can you pick up Clemmy after school and meet me at the laundry too?" Nobody questioned her. At least she wanted to do something, instead of waiting until it was too late.

At 3:45 the next afternoon me, my mother, Pete, Wash, Becky, Mrs. Taylor, and Mrs. Jackson stood in the front of the pressing club and felt very uncomfortable. Bama Jo walked in very businesslike, and before anyone could say anything, she said, "Mrs. Taylor, Mrs. Jackson, and Mrs. Campbell, I've asked people to do some brazen, often-times unreasonable things before in my life, and I have to admit I've asked a lot of selfish things of people before too, but I asked my new friends to meet me here this afternoon for one specific reason. Alex Campbell is going to die this November if somebody doesn't do something about it. Now I think it's high time for all of us to put aside any differences we may have. The man only did what he did because he loved some of you and he couldn't bear to see you hurt anymore. Now I've only known Alex for a week and a half but I know one thing, the world will be an empty place without him."

Everyone she talked to, including myself, felt a lump in the throat. "What can anyone do?" my mother asked shyly.

"I want Becky, Wash, and Luke to go with me to Atlanta tomorrow and I want your consent to get them out of school as many times as I need them until … well, you know until when. Pete, can you drive me tomorrow if they can go?"

At five o'clock the next morning we were on Highway 27 headed toward Atlanta. At eleven we saw the dome on top of the state capitol building. We walked up the gray steps to the main entrance doors. To me the glass-fronted doors with the large, worn brass handles, looked far bigger than any door I had ever seen. A uniformed guard stood next to the door. We followed Bama Jo through the doors and to the long reception desk on the right of the massive hall. Marble tile from North Georgia had paved the floor and had been used extensively everywhere I could see.

"I need to see the governor," she said sweetly to the first receptionist behind the counter.

"You can't simply walk in here and want to see the governor," the lady answered. "You need to make an appointment with his appointment secretary and it may be weeks or months before she will give you an audience."

"We don't have that long. Where is his appointment secretary?"

When we got to the office that supposedly contained this "appointment secretary," a short line was outside so Bama Jo took a number and we waited. At three o'clock that afternoon I was starving but we got to see the secretary.

The woman was thin and wore small wire-rimmed glasses, not too thick. She had gray hair with an occasional black strand pulled back fiercely into a small bun. She shouldn't have done it because her ears were big and should have been covered. "How may I help you?" She looked at Bama Jo and instant dislike clouded her face. How could anyone so pretty have anything to gripe to the governor about?

Bama Jo recognized the look and attacked first, using reason over emotion. "I know the governor is an awfully busy man but we need help." She explained in detail everything that happened. She saw the secretary's weak side and kept emphasizing the fact that this cold heartless man had continued to beat his wife.

Our appointment was for 4:30 that afternoon. We ran to the cafeteria and ate as fast as we could then came back and patiently waited in the appointment room a few steps away from the governor's office. I saw him coming down the hall surrounded by several busy-looking men a foot shorter than he was. He glanced in the open room where his appointments usually waited and nodded in our direction. I knew that he didn't remember. When we were summoned, I felt as if I were going to the principal's office for punishment. I was right.

Haltingly, Bama Jo tried to explain to the man what we were doing there. Wash got up and recited what the governor had told us that Sunday afternoon ten thousand years ago. He glanced at his watch then at the door guard. "I wish I could help you, but if I pardoned this man then every criminal in the state of Georgia would expect the same thing. I ran on a law-and-order campaign. Your friend broke the law."

"Sir. That girl Beth, Alex's daughter, hasn't spoken a word or recognized a soul since that day. She'd be dead if Alex hadn't stopped that man."

"Miss, never mind. Show them out, sergeant." The guard showed us out.

Bama Jo was mad. I felt empty. Pete was waiting in the car for us and I knew that if we went out there he would take us directly home. Several reporters were waiting for five o'clock. This was when the governor's work day would be over and he always enjoyed stopping and talking with the reporters. Get your name in the paper.

Bama Jo walked to the bench where five reporters sat or stood and smoked and waited. "You guys want a good story?" The pretty woman couldn't have come at a better time. The gubernatorial race was over for all practical purposes and everything would be ho-hum until the general election, and that wouldn't even be shown priority. A Republican couldn't win in the deep South.

She told the story in its entirety, leaving nothing out. The reporters wrote, their fingers flying. They asked me and Wash questions.

When the governor walked past the reporters, they looked at him distastefully. No one even bothered to ask him a question.

At midnight that night we got home. Nobody but Pete had been awake for hours. The next day in the newspapers, as Pete would say, the shit hit the fan. The Atlanta newspaper had pictures of me, Wash, and Becky on the front page. On the same page was a file picture of the governor with the caption "Governor breaks promise to three children." The full story followed, leaving out nothing. It was after school and the three of us were at the train station excitedly reading the story.

Alex was upset that we did what we did. Pete thought it was a good idea. Bama Jo told Alex that she didn't give a damn if it made him mad, but the rest of us weren't going to sit on our rear ends like he sat on his sanctimonious rear end, and do nothing.

"Spare me the sermon. There's nothing anyone can do if he won't pardon me."

"We have to make him see his error. He will brush this newspaper coverage aside because he knows the Atlanta papers don't like him anyway. We'll have to keep the pressure on him." She ignored Alex and directed her speech to the rest of us.

"How we going to do that, Bama Jo?" R.E.L. Carlton asked.

"When these fellows came to visit me in Florida, we started playing around each night singing and playing music. And to be perfectly candid, we sounded really good. By the fourth night everyone in town was on my front lawn listening. Have you got a big flatbed truck, Mr. Carlton?"

"Yes, ma'am, and you can have it if I get to drive."

"Will you go get it, sir, and load the piano on it while I see if we can borrow a loudspeaker system? We need to fix it so that the piano won't get wet when we go from place to place though. Can you handle that, Mr. Carlton?"

"Yes, ma'am. I can even get some loudspeakers if you want me to."

"What are you thinking about doing, Bama Jo?" Pete asked.

"We're going to play in the park this evening. If what I propose to do doesn't work here, it won't work in Atlanta or anyplace else, but if it works here, then I want every one of you to promise that you'll see this through. Is that a deal?"

"I'm not going to make a deal until you tell me what you're planning." Alex stuck his jaw out.

"You're going to have to wait until after this is over tonight."

Chapter Fifteen

I HAD NO IDEA WHERE HE GOT THE EQUIPMENT, but three hours later a grinning Mayor Carlton drove up with a flatbed truck with four big morning-glory-shaped speakers attached to the side rails and a piano-sized control box sitting behind the cab. While we marveled over the speaker system, Mr. Linwood and a helper from the hardware store drove up and started attaching floor flanges to the truck body. They screwed threaded pipe into the six flanges then screwed T-joints and forty-five-degree elbows onto the upright pipes. In a matter of minutes a hip-roofed skeleton was in place, needing only a canvas to cover it up.

"It'll be tomorrow morning before old man Hargrove gets through sewing the canvas top to this contraption," Mr. Carlton said proudly.

"Who knows how to operate this loudspeaker thingamajig?" Mr. O. Z. asked.

"These are the speakers they use over in Trinity at the football stadium. Took me a while, but I finally outwrestled the coach over there for them. He said he'd be here before sundown to show us how to use them."

True to his word, the burly coach got there and helped set up the microphones on the flatbed. He fooled with dials on the black control box and tested the microphones. At sundown Mr. O. Z. stepped up to the front microphone, and his saxophone filled the quiet night with the sweet strains of, "There will be peace." The piano softly joined then the guitar and the harmonica. On the second verse Bama Jo sang and her voice sounded just as I imagined the angels would sound when they sang.

The four corners of the small park were dimly lit by low-amp street lamps, but I saw them coming. One or two drifted up at first. They stood away, not realizing what was going on, then several more people joined them and they got closer. The night was still and sound carried easily. The sweet, mature, aroma of harvest time permeated the air of early night. At the end of the second song fifty people stood tentatively on the periphery of the truck where we played. They clapped haltingly at first then quit almost as if they were embarrassed.

We played and Bama Jo sang for almost an hour. A crowd had filled the park. Small children who where unruly were quickly sat down and told to shut up. Grown men hummed or clapped along with the music and after each song ended whistles and applause exploded.

She was a natural. She picked up the microphone and waited until the crowd was completely silent. "We're glad you came and we're so happy that you enjoyed yourselves. Thank you from the bottom of my heart. Now it's time to ask you to do a favor for us. The governor promised Luke, and Becky, and Wash, these three children on this truck, that he would pardon Alex for what he did. Now any decent person knows that it isn't right for a man to beat his wife. I want each of you to write a letter to the governor tomorrow morning telling him that you're not voting for him come election day if he doesn't keep his promise. Will you do this for us?" They clapped and cheered and yelled "yes" and "we're behind you" for thirty minutes. They gathered around the truck and cheered. They wouldn't stop.

Bama Jo turned to face everyone on the truck. "Get a good night's sleep. We're going to Atlanta tomorrow. Can you drive the truck, Mr. Carlton?"

"Yes ma'am, Bama Jo."

"No drinking, Mr. Carlton?"

"No ma'am. I won't touch a drop."

Mr. O. Z. called his boss at the Central of Georgia Railroad that night and told them to send a temporary replacement. Mayor Carlton met his sawmill crew at five o'clock the next morning as he always did and appointed the biggest man to be in charge while he was gone. He explained in explicit language what he would do to each of them if they failed to work hard or refused to obey his new foreman. Alex woke Chilie and explained what needed to be done on the farm and left knowing the man would get it done. At 6:30 A.M. Alex's big car headed north with the flatbed truck close behind. Alex, Bama Jo, and Pete sat in the front seat. Mr. O. Z. and John Smith argued in the back. Me, Wash, and Becky rode in the big truck with Mr. Carlton.

We checked into the Biltmore on West Peachtree Street that afternoon at two o'clock. The parking lot attendant hadn't wanted to let the big truck park in the hotel parking lot until Mr. Carlton got out and stood over the small man and explained. "You might not let me park in here but I'm going to explain to you what's going to happen to you if any of the equipment on this truck is stolen." The attendant had a change of heart.

The three of us were in awe. We had never seen buildings this tall or so many people and cars. Taxis were everywhere, and people by the thousands walked on the sidewalks always in a hurry. I thought that a man could live on this spot and never have to go over a block to do anything he ever wanted. I nudged Wash. "I may move here instead of going to Montana."

"Ain't no trains to rob up here. I'm still going to Montana."

Bama Jo questioned one of the hotel clerks on duty, and within the hour she had hired a car with double loudspeakers on top to drive her wherever she needed. This afternoon she had decided to set up and play at an empty lot midway between the Biltmore and the Fox theater. The lot was clean and well packed and a construction company sign stood in one corner next to the sidewalk but construction hadn't begun. The lot was large, it fronted on Peachtree Street, and went almost back to the next street. I asked her did we have permission to play there. "Honey, it's far easier to get forgiveness than to get permission. Just think about all the sins people commit. They would never get permission from the Lord to commit them but he always forgives them after the fact."

She got permission from the shop owner next door to run an electrical cord to the truck, and at quarter to five Mr. O. Z. put his saxophone close to the front microphone and "Amazing Grace" stopped the passing people dead in their tracks. In fifteen minutes the lot couldn't hold another person.

We played and she sang two more songs then she picked up the microphone and spoke to the crowd with her clear sweet voice that sounded kind of sad and kind of happy at the same time. "Ladies and gentlemen, my name is Bama Jo Austin. I won't take but a minute of your time. This is Alex Campbell and he killed his son-in-law in cold blood because he beat his daughter so bad that she slipped into a catatonic state and hasn't recovered. Now the governor came to South Georgia this summer campaigning and Becky and her two friends Wash and Luke, who is Alex's grandson, met the governor and he promised to pardon Alex." She paused. "Now he refuses to keep his promise. What I would ask of you is to write him and tell him that you aren't going to vote for any man who breaks his promises. Will you do that for me?"

They went crazy. Angry cries and applause mixed with yells and mild oaths continued for several minutes. Somewhere in the back I saw several men fighting. Bama Jo asked for silence and complete order was restored. She worked the crowd like a professional. "We are going to play our songs an hour before sundown in Ansley Park. We don't have permission but maybe some of you would come and, if we get arrested, please get us out of jail. Friday at noon before the governor leaves for the weekend, we are going to start at the Peachtree Sovthern Railroad Station at Brookwood and walk to the Capitol. Will you join us when we come by?" Again the crowd yelled and screamed.

The shop owner came out his back door and approached the truck. Most of the crowd was gone but many were still around our truck offering support or money or to help physically if needed. They were told again and again that money wasn't needed. Support and prayers were what we needed. The shop owner was a slight man with a stern and unsmiling face. He looked directly at me but I knew he was talking to Alex. "I've got a daughter too and I'd kill any man who beat her too. I know a couple of city commissioners. I'll see to it that they are there tonight in case you have trouble with the police." He nodded and walked back to his store and his shoulders were square, not drooped anymore, and his step had more spring in it than I figured it had had in years. "I'll arrange some electricity for you over at the park." He said as he closed his back door.

We hurried to the sandwich shop next door and wolfed down the quickest thing they offered on the limited menu. Bama Jo got in the front seat with the driver of the loud speaker car and as we followed her slowly down the crowded street she invited Peachtree Street to a free concert in the park. When we arrived at the park several hundred people were already there. Some spoke as if they were old friends. Some waved. They all smiled sadly. A bond had formed and they were committed. I wondered if at some time in their lives they had gone through something that made them identify with our cause. I wondered how many of them had been beaten by a drunk man they called father or a brutal man they had mistakenly married.

Some men stood straight with there thumbs up to show their support. Some women dabbed their eyes. I saw several men in wide brimmed hats carrying cameras, and I knew that the newspaper would make the governor's breakfast go uneaten or undigested the next morning.

Our new friend Mr. Pemberton, the shop owner, walked through the people toward our position. He wore a World War I–vintage army uniform. The insignia that announced he had been a one-star general was displayed on his shoulders and cap. Battle ribbons filled the left chest of his coat. In his wake were two men, who looked to be about his age, dressed in suits and ties. "Evening, folks. These two were officers in my command in the first war. Damn good officers, I might add. They're city commissioners now but we still try to fight the common enemy." He turned and said, "Right men?"

"Yes sir, general," They answered.

"I closed my store until you folks leave town. I'm at your service and these men are too."

I had heard Bama Jo's story several times, and each time it affected me the same way. A tightening of the chest and throat and my eyes stinging and overflowing. She was a master, but she was such a sincere master and she never asked her audience for anything but understanding and support. Dozens of people had offered money but they were politely told each time by Bama Jo to give it to a charity that supported battered women and children. She sang prettier that night in the park than I had ever heard. Thousands of people silently sat on the ground or stood on the periphery listening to her uncommon voice. The softness of a saxophone, piano, guitar, harmonica, and three tambourines filled out the lapse in her songs but there wasn't any doubt that she was the show. She was what made them blink their eyes. She made their throats feel funny.

"I want each of you to think about something very carefully. Alex witnessed this little girl's father abuse her and her mother for years. He finally had the man put in prison for a long time and then he was faced with his only daughter being abused by her husband. He couldn't take it any more and he killed the man. His fate is in your hands. Only the people can make the governor see that we don't want these monsters living in our midst. The Lord forgave Alex the instant he killed that man because it broke his heart too when he saw this beautiful child Becky with her arm dangling and broken and he saw Beth staring ahead now but seeing nothing. Will you help me right this wrong? Will you help us send a message to our governor?"

The next two days were a whirlwind. Thousands of people. Morning, noon, and night they came and listened to our songs and listened to Bama Jo's sweet voice tell her story. The general and his two officers had been joined by a cast of fifty or sixty, each paused from their normal routine to join the commerce we pursued until we were finished. "You are my soldiers of good fortune and I adore you for it." She told them and each would have bit his own arm off for her. We hit the parks and public places and never once got asked if we had a permit. Downtown, not far from the Coca-Cola sign was a small pedestrian park. Friday morning at 7:30 Mr. O. Z. stepped to the microphone and began his song and pigeons flew. In thirty minutes four thousand people stood silently and listened to Bama Jo.

At eleven o'clock we started the long walk to the capitol. Each of us held a sign that read, "Pardon Alex Campbell." The press was there in droves. Since Wednesday night we had made front page in both Atlanta papers and probably several of the surrounding publications. The newspaper that touted that it "Covers Dixie Like the Dew" was on our side. They quoted Bama Jo extensively, and everyone knew what we were doing and knew that we were walking down Peachtree toward the Capitol on Friday.

We started on the sidewalk, fifty or sixty of us. People stood and watched us go by. Some nodded and said, "Good luck Alex." some said they prayed for him, some wept. Some had their hats off, some reached to touch his hand. They all fell in line behind us. No one was loud, no one disorderly. Some had signs saying to pardon Alex, some carried the American flag. Becky cried and Alex swept her up in his arms and never missed a step. Closed signs appeared on shops as we walked by and merchants locked their doors and joined the back of the line. The street was full of people now and oncoming traffic had stopped. Some got out of their cars and joined the people marching. John Smith popped his harmonica against the heel of his hand and blew a marching tune.

We were an odd lot walking down Peachtree Street. Three strong willed men from the country, one black drayman who had been elevated to the stars, three kids, one of them being carried by the man who sent her father to prison, a big man who would fight the meanest and baddest but was afraid of my grandfather, and a woman who made a city stop and listen. We were an odd lot indeed. Policemen on call boxes alerted policemen ahead so that traffic could be diverted around our street and no one seemed to mind. Second-, third-, and fourth-floor windows were raised as we walked past and people called for Bama Jo and Alex. One old man in a wheel chair wearing and old army uniform waited for us on a corner then tried to keep up. Pete walked over to the edge of the street where the man was furiously working his arms. "Hold on, mate, and I'll push you. I was in the army too."

Old ladies with canes joined in and walked until they couldn't. Young housewives pushed trams with babies that they didn't want beaten and abused ever. Soldiers just home from the recent war joined us because they wanted to belong again. We were an army and the enemy had better listen. Our troops were marching on and election day would be when we stopped.

When we passed the Imperial Hotel, the street curved a little and began to climb. I looked behind us and people were following as far as I could see. The last few blocks Bama Jo held my and Wash's hand. Mayor Carlton tapped Pete on the shoulder and took the push handles of the wheel chair. Becky was walking with Alex holding tight to his hand.

He was waiting at the top of the steps. Flanked by forty state troopers he stood at his vantage point and watched the whole landscape fill with people. Side streets to the top of the hill where Rich's department store stood were filled with people. He didn't wait until all of the marchers could hear. "Ladies and gentlemen, I feel I need to explain my position on this matter. If I pardoned this criminal for first degree murder because he claims that he killed a man who was beating his wife then every murderer in the state of Georgia would use the same ploy."

Someone shouted, "Then we'll vote for your opponent."

"Be realistic. This is the Deep South. A Republican can't win."

Bama Jo asked if she could use his loudspeaker to answer him.

"This is not a debate. I'm sorry, young lady," he answered. She shouted, "If we can't trust you to keep your promise to these children then we can't trust you to run our state. We are going to try to add you to the ranks of the unemployed come November then governor."

Then he lost his temper and screamed back at her, "I don't care who the hell any of you vote for, I'm going to be your next governor."

The people who heard his remark booed and jeered. The press took thousands of pictures and the next day his last statement was splashed across the entire top of the front page in both major Atlanta newspapers. Thousands of hand-painted signs appeared on walls, in windows of businesses, taped to doors of automobiles, and every other conceivable place that someone might see. Each sign professed a strong dislike for the governor, or pledged support for Alex.

Fifty to sixty of the people who had been with us since we started our campaign in Atlanta met at General Pemberton's shop on Saturday morning. We were packed and ready to go to Augusta. The general organized the group as if they were on a military maneuver. He divided them by the section of the city they lived in, then he named district captains. In one short hour he had an organization in place dedicated to keeping the fire going. The group was verging on fanaticism by the time we waved our good-byes. Bama Jo had hugged each of the people there and more than one grown man dabbed at his eyes or blew his nose.

Saturday night we played our song in Augusta close to the bridge leading to South Carolina. On Sunday we went to the largest Baptist church in Augusta and the minister recognized us and asked the congregation to join him in a prayer for our effort. Sunday afternoon and evening were much like Atlanta only smaller. The Baptist minister called on the local ministerial association and all the churches canceled church that night and joined us. When we left Augusta on Monday morning the ministers had started a grassroots organization that would bring the governor to Augusta in three weeks to try and save his following.

Monday afternoon found us in Savannah. The Mulberry Hotel, located at Abercorn and Bay Streets, was the best hotel in the area. The manager came to greet us when we registered. "I've read about you and what you're doing. Although I don't disagree with you, the policy at the Mulberry Hotel is to stay neutral in all things of controversy. We do not want huge crowds disturbing our guests. Am I making myself clear?"

Mr. O. Z. spoke up before anyone else had a chance to rebut. "If we cause you any economic harm then we'll leave. However, if you're asking us not to register to stay in your hotel then we'll play on the sidewalk in front of the damned door. Am I making myself clear?"

We played that night across Bay Street in the park in front of Factors Walk near the river. The lonesome horn of an incoming ship called for the tiny tugboats that would slip through the darkness and gently nudge it to its berth upriver. The tiny carrying the mighty. The weak slaying the strong. I remembered my Sunday school teacher reading Ecclesiastes. "I returned and under the sun I saw that the race did not always go to the swift, nor the battle to the strong." The nine that had placed their backs to the river and played a swan song were the weak. No matter how strong Mayor Carlton was or how pretty Bama Jo sang or how she moved people with her story of Alex, we were the meek, and even though we might be blessed and eventually might inherit the earth as the Bible proclaimed, we faced a task that seemed to be overwhelming us.

Drunk sailors with boylike faces came from the bars that lined the brick road next to the river. The dark faces of the Geechee blacks that sold their handmade wares in the old slave market stared from the outer perimeter of people gathering and listening.

She did something different tonight because she suspected

that the liquor that flowed in the hot-blooded veins of the young sailors might create a problem. "I want to tell you why we are here tonight. Then if you want us to leave just tell us and we'll go." One drunk boy in uniform jeered when she finished her story but a much larger boy dressed in the same white uniform picked him up by his collar until their eyes met and the drunk boy had a change of heart. The taverns that lined the river front didn't have a customer so the barkeeps sat on the rails that kept their customers from falling in the river and listened. Mr. O. Z. was getting better and better. He was making his horn almost speak when two black and white cars stopped where the crowd spilled over into the street and eight big policemen with billy sticks walked to the flatbed truck where we were.

"Do you have a permit for this?" the lead man, with three gold stripes on his sleeve, asked.

"Do you need a permit in the city to sing?" Bama Jo asked the man.

"Don't get smart with me, lady. Answer the question."

"No sir. We don't have a permit to sing."

"This is an assembly in the streets. The same as a parade. I've got to make a case against you."

She persisted, "Mister, all we did was park our truck in this parking space, which is not illegal, and we started playing and singing, which is not illegal. These kind people stopped to listen, which is not illegal. I imagine some of these brave boys and millions of other people have been fighting for the past several years to change those laws."

"Get off the truck, lady. You're under arrest."

The big blonde boy that had shown his shipmate proper

manners walked over and looked down at the cop. "If you want to arrest anyone arrest me and my shipmates."

"Don't get in this, son. We don't want to arrest you, only the lady." Pete and Alex were virtually holding Mr. Carlton back by now. About a hundred young men in sailor uniforms had walked up behind their comrade in arms.

The fair-haired boy answered the police sergeant. "Mister, I'm from Nebraska and my folks moved there from Germany after the first war to get away from people like you. I think that the man Alex Campbell has been done wrong by your kind and we're going to listen as long as the lady talks and sings. Now you can sit down and shut up, or you can go back to where ever you came from, or you are going to get the hell beat out of you." The boy never raised his voice, but I knew that we were about to see our first trouble since we started this mission.

The cop motioned toward his platoon and with a mighty swing aimed for the tall sailor's head. His momentum carried him halfway around when his billy stick didn't hit anything but air. He woke up two hours later with a big fist print on his jaw. "The rest of you sit down and listen," the farm boy from Nebraska told the open-mouthed cops.

We stayed in Savannah for three days, and the chief of police sent men with us everywhere we went. He didn't miss one of Bama Jo's songs after his men told him what we did. When we started to leave he led us through the city with his siren blaring. He told Alex that morning. "My father was what the Queen called the Black Irish. He got the taste of strong drink from his mother's milk and never learned to master the stuff. He beat me too. God bless you, Alex Campbell."

Brunswick came, and the golden islands of Georgia, where the rich had played before Mr. Flagler built his railroad that would take them to Miami. We were picking up steam. Waycross, where all the trains that traveled the southern seaboard crossed tracks. Valdosta, where the men who had flown through unfriendly skies last year were quietly planning for a confrontation with the country they called a bear. The last town, where the Chattahoochee met the Flint, then home to my mother and Lucy's cooking. We had been gone for two weeks and the election was four weeks away the next Tuesday.

Wednesday and Thursday, me, Wash, and Becky went to school while the rest of our group planned and got their business in order. Mr. Roy held a barbecue at his service station to raise money for our trips to come. He told Alex, "I know that you don't accept charity, and I know that you will not tell a lie, but all I'm giving you is the profits from the event. Goddammit, Alex, take the money."

We drove to Columbus that Saturday morning. Bama Jo wanted to go to every medium-sized city within a day's drive of Chickasaw. The University of Georgia and Auburn University were playing their annual football game that afternoon at one o'clock. Alex told us, "There's very few things I would rather do than try to keep me out of the electric chair but this is one of those things. We're going to the football game this afternoon. I haven't missed one of these games in twenty years."

He bought tickets from a scalper a block away from the stadium and borrowed a wheelchair from the stadium office. "They aren't going to let John Smith in the game unless we disguise him. Pete, get in the wheelchair and let John Smith push you in."

"Alex, I don't mind doing what I can to save you from the electric chair but I'll be damned if I'm going to let John Smith push me up to the top of the stadium where our seats are. I know deep down in his heart he wants to kill me and he might take this opportunity."

"I'll get in the chair," Becky told Alex.

We watched the ball game, then played our songs at Lakebottom Park.

Chapter Sixteen

OR TWO WEEKS WE TRAVELED A CLOSE CIRCUIT, near enough to go home each night. We were building a base of support that was respectable, but whether it was enough to do any good, only time would tell. Bama Jo had told us hundreds of times that the only way to get the governor to pardon Alex was to convince him that he would win in November only with our support. The prospects looked dismal, if not impossible. We came home to rest for a few days before we began our final swing that would end in Atlanta for a full week of campaigning against the governor before the general election.

The only person who was truly happy was the Republican candidate, even though the newspapers were giving him a one-in-three chance of winning if the election were held now. He made several attempts to join us as we traveled, but Bama Jo always rejected his invitations. Once when a newspaper reporter was interviewing her, he asked why we weren't ever seen with the Republican candidate. "We are not campaigning for anyone. We are campaigning against the governor. If he pardons Alex, then we will quit campaigning against him."

The comment made headlines, but I don't think that it had any impact on the governor.

Miss Sadie was the postmistress of Chickasaw. She got Chilie to bring her a fifty-gallon wooden barrel with one end removed. It was almost full of letters addressed to Alex before we left for our last attempt to change the governor's mind. The newspaper-reading public in the state of Georgia was beginning to take a very active interest in what we were doing. We became a force to be reckoned with—something that might mean the difference between a landslide in November and a squeak-by. We made our way from town to town almost mechanically. Most of the time I couldn't remember where we were and didn't really care. Each of us smiled less frequently. No one argued except Mr. O. Z. and John Smith. Each passing day without positive news made us more acutely aware that Alex's Armageddon was coming. November thirtieth was looming larger.

We were home for three days the week before the election. Sheriff Gaines drove into our yard at eight o'clock on Sunday morning. I saw him when he got out of his car, and I knew that he wasn't making a friendly social call. He looked up at the blue morning sky then twisted each side of his waxed mustache before he shook his head sadly and slowly walked toward the front door. Alex had seen him too. Before the sheriff could knock, Alex opened the door and said, "Morning, Sheriff. I don't imagine you drove over here for a cup of coffee. Let's have it."

"Somebody from Atlanta called my office and told me that the governor was considering invoking his power to suspend me as sheriff if I didn't obey the law and put you in jail until your execution date."

"And . . ."

"And I'm not going to put you in jail, because if I did I would face a write-in candidate in the election that would probably beat me. I'm going to put you under house arrest. Alex, I can't let you go out of this county any more. If the Georgia State Troopers see you again, they have orders to send you straight to Reidsville until the thirtieth."

"What about the Atlanta police. Have they got orders too?"

"Nope. The mayor up there is on your side, but you aren't planning to go there, are you?"

"When do you want me to be there? I'm fairly certain that bastard in Atlanta isn't going to pardon me."

"You need to be at the state prison on the fifteenth."

"I'll be there."

"Alex, why don't you leave? No one would even look for you."

"I think you know the answer to that."

"Alex, did I ever tell you about me fighting with Teddy Roosevelt in the Spanish-American war? That's when I decided I wanted to be a sheriff."

"No."

"Well, I made every step he made up San Juan Hill, fighting every foot of the way. Men lay dying everywhere. When we captured that hill and planted a flag there old Teddy told me, 'Sergeant Gaines, this is a great and historic thing we have done today. People all over the United States are going to hear about us. When we get home we'll ride in parades and drink iced tea all over Washington. I think either me or you ought to run for president.' I told him right then and there, 'Why don't you run for president? All I want to be is sheriff of Chickasaw County, Georgia.' That's all I ever wanted to be Alex. Now I'm through. I'm a-quitting. I don't want to be sheriff anymore. I'll finish up the sorry mess what you're going through, then I'm finished."

"That would be a shame. You would have been a better President than Teddy and you sure as hell are a better sheriff than that little pissant running against you ever will be."

The first Tuesday in November was five days away when we went back to Atlanta. General Pemberton and his army were waiting. They had done their job. They had the enemy trying to recover lost bastions of support while they weakened other positions. The general attacked offensively, always using his forces to hit a particular neighborhood and completely saturate it with our message. Churches, fire stations, police precincts, sand-lot baseball games, anything to get the people talking and on our side. They had made hundreds of signs demanding Alex's freedom and attached them to tall slats. Volunteers carried the signs petitioning for Alex's pardon everywhere people congregated. Electric trolleys that roamed the main streets of Atlanta frequently played host to the hand-painted signs. Some operators left the signs on until the cleaning crew took them off.

The general wasn't as squeamish about taking money as we were. He had a sizable bank account started from contributions and wanted to broadcast a radio message immediately. He and Bama Jo went to the oldest and most-listened-to radio station in the city and taped several thirty-second messages. Alex had objected to the expense but fell silent when the general reasoned that the money couldn't be returned now anyway. He didn't keep a record of who contributed.

∂❧

We played our songs three times each day—at noon, close to the places where large crowds of people would be at lunch, at five o'clock to catch people getting off work, and early evening closer to movie theaters or other attractions that were frequented at night. Alex had asked General Pemberton to get someone to keep watch for police or state troopers, and when he was warned he would slip into the crowd.

The Biltmore's main lobby was where everyone congregated when we weren't working or sleeping. The hotel staff, even the maids, knew us and went to extra lengths to help in any way possible. A large radio, taller than I, was there for the benefit of anyone who wanted to listen. The news came on at nine each night, and we usually stayed up until after it had gone off the air before going to bed. The governor had bought air time each night before the news came on. Each of the three nights before the election he explained his position on not pardoning Alex and the station programmer, who must have been on our side, played Bama Jo's husky voice explaining our side immediately after.

The radio news announcer each night was a man named Edward Horsley who was also part-owner of the station. At some point in his broadcast each night the campaign we were waging came up in his nightly comment: "Ladies and gentlemen the gadflies from South Georgia are in the governor's ointment. We might see a Republican governor in the Deep South this year. It could very well be the best thing that ever happened to our fair state. It would be a pleasant experience not to have any new bills passed for a while. We taxpayers have to check our pockets after the legislature convenes each year to see how much more of our money those scoundrels have spent, and I for one have had enough. I wish you well, Alex Campbell."

By lunchtime Monday everyone realized that any hope that the governor would pardon Alex at the last minute was gone. The chances of electing a Republican were slim, and even if the man won, Alex's date with the electric chair would come before the new governor took office. Mayor Carlton told us, "Looks to me like we're between a rock and a hard place. I think Bama Jo needs to release me from my promise not to drink whiskey. As low as I feel today, if I had some of Lonnie's stuff to sharpen my wits, I'd figure a way to kill the bastard. Excuse me for saying that, Bama Jo, but sometimes you've got to call a spade a spade and a bastard a bastard." She walked to the big man's side and squeezed his shoulder. "I think he's a bastard too."

Alex said it was time for us to go home. He had a catch in his voice. "I didn't know that a man could be blessed with friends like you people are. We gave it our best shot, but the governor isn't going to pardon me and I've got to get some things in order and the rest of you need to do the same."

"I think we need to stay through tomorrow and go to the main polling places," Mr. O. Z. said to Alex.

"Why? All we were trying to do was get the man to change his mind. We weren't trying to beat him."

Pete said to no one in particular, "Well the way I feel about it wouldn't stand much scrutiny by the ministerial association.

I've only got one leg, but I'd damn near give it to see that cracker governor unemployed."

"I still think the bastard needs killing."

"Me too," Becky added.

The mayor said, "It seems to me we might have gone coon hunting and our dogs treed a bear. When you do that, all's that's left to do is call off the dogs and piss on the fire and go home."

"What are you going to do, Alex?" Pete asked.

"I guess I'll go home and dust off the family Bible and see if the Lord remembers me. Looks as if I'm going to be introduced to him in a few weeks."

"Well, at least you won't be running into Reuben up there." Pete added.

Bama Jo was mad. "I'm not giving up, and damn you spineless men, you aren't either. Let's go home and plan a new strategy."

The next morning I had to go back to school. Our teacher took a straw vote and the Republican got all the class votes. That day at seven the polls closed and I wandered by the old two-story Mason hall where the people in the city limits cast their votes. The people I had traveled with and grown to love over the past few weeks were sitting in the bandstand across the park from the polling place. Alex was the only one conspicuously absent. No one smiled at me when I walked up and flopped down on a bench. "Who's winning?" I asked.

"Don't know yet," Wash answered. "Becky, it's your turn to go see."

"Go with me, Luke," she directed.

We walked up the narrow steps and into the humming room. One of the ladies posting results as the readers called them looked up and smiled at me. "No one has voted for the governor yet," she told me.

We walked back across the park toward the bandstand. Becky had circled her arms over her head in the shape of an O. "Satisfactory," Mayor Carlton said. "I wish I could catch him down here again. I'd leave him in Echowah swamp but I figure the alligators would turn up their nose at him."

"Puke him out if they did eat him," Wash said.

At nine o'clock the poll workers posted the results. Six hundred eighty four for the Republican, two votes for the incumbent. "My guess is that those two votes were mistakes," the poll lady said before bidding us a good night. General Pemberton called Wednesday morning before I went to school. My mother answered the phone and called Alex from the breakfast table. "Alex, a Mr. Pemberton is on the phone and says it's important. You might warn him that Sister Ruby is probably listening if the call is personal."

"It can't be that personal. I don't mind." He picked up the receiver and stuck it to his ear before he picked up the tall speaking part of the telephone. "Morning, General. Morning, Sister Ruby."

After he talked for a few minutes then hung up, he sat back down to breakfast. "The general said the Republican beat the governor in Atlanta. He said from what he can gather though, the towns around that we didn't visit are coming in for the Democrat."

Pete said, "If we had started two months earlier, we could have beat him soundly. Might still do it."

It was a long day for all of us. Late that afternoon the big cabinet radio in the parlor of our house announced that the preliminary results were 51 percent for the incumbent, 49 percent for the challenger. The announcer sounded bitter. "I'm going against station policy to only report the news and not take sides with what I'm about to say, but there comes a time when a man's got to say what he thinks needs saying. God bless you, Alex Campbell, if by chance you happen to be listening and if your group starts a recall petition to oust the governor, stop by this station and I'll be the first to sign it."

The telephone rang. I answered the phone this time. It was Bama Jo. "Tell your grandpa we need to start a recall petition."

I couldn't go to sleep right away that night so I silently left my room and started for the kitchen. Lights were coming from under the door of the parlor. I noiselessly cracked the door and Alex sat in a high-backed wing chair next to a reading lamp. His back was to the door and didn't see me. He was reading the big Bible. He looked up and closed the book, leaving it in his lap. "God, I realize that I haven't been much of a son for you to brag about. I've even gone through times when I didn't appreciate your decisions very much. When you took my Mary Beth and then my son Alex I guess I didn't understand that, and I apologize for doubting your wisdom then. It seems like me and you are fixing to meet face to face and I'd like to ask you to forgive me for all my shortcomings before I turn my fate over to you. I'd like to leave this earth with a full tank on a smooth road. Lord, you know for a fact that I have never cheated another human being or stole in my life. You also know that I haven't told a lie since I was a small child other than the things I told the Judge, and that wasn't bearing false witness against anyone but myself. The fact is, Lord, without you thinking that I'm patting myself on the back too much, I never broke any of your commandments. I'd appreciate if you took that into consideration come the thirtieth of this month. Amen. In case you don't remember me, my name is Alex Campbell, and before I go tonight I'd like to ask you to see after Beth, and Clementine and my grandson after I'm gone."

I silently closed the door feeling funny for having eavesdropped on Alex praying. I dreamed about my father's funeral that night and I dreamed about Alex dressed up in a priest's collar and robe with angel wings on his back.

"Alex, we've got to try a recall election. We can't sit here and do nothing," Bama Jo beseeched Alex early the next morning at our breakfast table. Pete had already gone for the day.

"Bama Jo. Today is Thursday. Two weeks from this Sunday coming up the state is going to execute me. I told Sheriff Grimes that I would be in Reidsville day after tomorrow, and that's what I'm going to do. What can we do in two weeks?"

"By damn, we can try to the end. That's what we can do. Alex, you have become a very special friend and I am not going to quit. I'm going back to Atlanta Monday and beg on my hands and knees for him to pardon you."

"You can't go up there by yourself, my lady friend. Just give it up."

"I'm not going by myself. When you turn yourself in Saturday night, Pete gets his bond money back. He said he was going with me to offer the governor the fifty thousand dollars to pardon you."

"I'm going too." I stared Alex and my mother down.

"No, you are not. You've skipped enough school," my mother said, not too convincingly.

"Yes, I am. He's my grandpa, and I'm going."

Alex disappeared that morning after breakfast and didn't come home until Saturday noon. Becky came by and mentioned that her mother had to leave town on business and wouldn't be home until Saturday afternoon. I secretly wished that Alex would catch a bus to South America and call us all to join him.

On Saturday afternoon Alex spent a long time with Beth, talking to her low and holding her hands, then he got Pete and me to drive him to Colonel Ferguson's office. The old lawyer was waiting with a briefcase full of papers for him to sign. Alex was a wealthy man and his estate had to be left in order. Before Alex became a prisoner of the state, he asked Pete if he would mind being the administrator of his estate, then he had squatted so he could look me in the eyes and said, "You've got to be a man now, Luke. See to your mother and mind her. Pete will be with you to give you good advice and promise me you won't ever do anything either of us would be ashamed of you for." He hugged me, then he stood up and looked his old adversary in the eye. Two old men hugged each other and didn't say anything. I looked at them and I don't think either of them could have spoken at that time. We took him to the drugstore and waited until the big red and silver Trailways bus pulled up. Alex glanced back toward us one time, then boarded the bus that would take him to his death.

Chapter Seventeen

WHEN WE GOT HOME, Pete called the sheriff. "He didn't want to cause you any inconvenience, Gaines. I know he was supposed to turn himself in to you. He said he'd pay his own way over to Reidsville."

That night at supper me, Pete, and my mother pushed our food around and didn't talk very much at all. Shortly after the meal Pete excused himself and said he was going to bed. My mother told me that she had a headache and went to bed after warning me that I would go to Sunday school and church tomorrow, no excuses accepted.

Wash came by at eight the next morning. He asked me if I wanted him to go to church with me. "Where were you yesterday?" he asked. "Becky spent the night with me and my mama Friday night and we looked for you." I told him about me and Pete driving Alex to catch the bus.

"Why didn't he get off the bus at the crossroads and head for Montana?"

"I asked him why he didn't run away, and he told me he gave the sheriff his word that he'd be in Reidsville when he was supposed to."

The preacher had chiseled his sermon finely. He spoke of the Old Testament. He was preaching to the congregation but talking to me and my mother. In his own way he was trying to comfort us, but he made me uncomfortable. He explained that the laws Moses had brought down from Mount Sinai were God's rules for life, but could be forgiven, but only if the sinner was genuinely remorseful and prayed for forgiveness. I wanted to run as fast as I could away from that church. When the preacher started telling us again how a person could be forgiven for taking another's life I couldn't sit there anymore. I bolted from my mother's side and left her and Wash sitting there to take the stares I knew were coming. I ran past Mayor Carlton as he nodded. I knew that Mr. O. Z. and Bama Jo were there watching. I wanted to find Pete and get him to drive me to the jail where Alex was. I wanted to make sure he was going to heaven.

She didn't fuss at me when she got home. She picked up my scattered Sunday clothes and hung them in their proper place. Me and Wash rode the mules Alex had given us to Alex's farm that afternoon. Tall trees canopied the road leading to the land my grandpa loved. The November frosts had painted the leaves bright reds, and yellows, and oranges. One particular hardwood grove on Alex's farm looked as if God were trying out his paint palate when he colored these trees. I remembered when my mother had asked Alex to go to church with us a few weeks prior. "Clementine, you and Luke go with me to my church today. You wouldn't believe the cathedral he made for me on the farm. Biggest stand of hardwood trees you've ever seen and they are showing off now. Brightest colors you've ever seen. I don't believe any person in his right mind could walk through those trees and not hear God calling." I knew that I had found Alex's cathedral. These woods were Alex's church.

Mayor Carlton drove his big Buick into our yard at seven the next morning and blew his horn. Bama Jo and Mr. O. Z. were in the front seat with him. O. Z. had told the two of them several times that this trip would be wasted. The governor was mad as hell with us and probably wouldn't even see us.

"He will see us," Bama Jo told him. "The general is going to meet us with half the radio and newspaper people in Atlanta in tow."

Me and Pete left to meet them, and as we walked to the car the front door opened, and my mother said, "Wait. Can I go too? I mean, I'm going too."

When we walked up the long flight of steps leading to the front door of the Capitol, Mr. Pemberton was there waiting. Twenty or thirty people with cameras or press cards or both waited around the entrance for us. Today was different from the first time. When we walked to the main reception desk, the clerk picked up the phone and spoke quietly. She hung up and said, "You know where his office is. He'll see you immediately."

He sat behind the huge desk. An American flag was on his right and a Georgia flag on his left. Four tall men in uniform flanked his desk and the big pistols on their belts made them seem even bigger than they were. Several rows of seats were there to accommodate visitors. Probably enough to hold thirty people. He allowed reporters to stand against the back wall after the seats were all taken. "Welcome to my office." He told us. "I want you all to know that I bear no grudge. I don't hold any animosity for any of you. You almost beat me fair and square and that is something even I admire." He smiled then chuckled. "I simply don't have the same latitude that the Lord has though. I can't forgive Alex. The law won't allow me. The state of Georgia has given me a set of laws to enforce and I took an oath to enforce them. Your Alex broke the Lord's law when he killed that man and he broke the state of Georgia's law."

Bama Jo went for the weak point. "I brought fifty thousand dollars for your next campaign. In cash."

The man seemed to wilt a little and his eyes darted about, first to the bodyguards then to Bama Jo's purse. He licked his lips as if mentally tasting an imaginary favorite meal, then distress clouded his features. I think he would have taken the money if no one had been around. "I can't pardon Alex."

My mother spoke, and all the emotions she had felt for months came through in her plea. "Come with us and see Beth, Alex's daughter. She was the most beautiful girl I've ever known and now she stares without seeing and drools on her bedclothes because of the monster she was married to. Just come see her."

We faced a silent governor. We went home.

We lived the rest of the week and on Sunday we dressed for church and Pete decided that it might not be such a bad idea if he went with me and my mother. He was dressed and waiting for us when we left the house. My mother looked puzzled when she saw him dressed in a suit. "Where are you going so dressed up?"

"I thought that I'd go to church with you and Luke. Won't hurt."

The church was filled to overflowing. Mrs. Jackson and Wash were walking down the side street. We waited until they intersected and stopped to exchange pleasantries. She talked to us, but she looked at Pete. When we walked into the church, she sat by Pete and I noticed that her leg touched his the entire service. The minister's final message to the crowded church was that the Methodist and Baptist church would have a joint service the following Sunday to ask God for a miracle in Alex's behalf. "We will ask God for favorable weather so that we may worship in the park. He, not seeing fit for us to worship in the park, we will try to fit us all into this house of worship since we can hold a few more that our sister church."

I rode my mule to Alex's farm that afternoon and lay in the tall broom sedge until the sun was low. Tall trees turned loose their brown leaves which floated to the earth in loose abandon. I wished that I was a grown man. I would break Alex out of Reidsville and take him to Mexico. I figured that if God didn't remember who Alex was two weeks ago he certainly had been reminded enough by now. Everybody I knew said they were praying for him. The sky had turned a soft pink when I rode my mule home feeling lonelier than I'd ever felt. A moon the color of fresh-churned butter was making its way toward the top of the sky.

I had skipped all the days allowable from school and I wasn't going back to face my class and the stares that came with it until I felt like it. My mother woke me on Monday, and I got dressed as if I were going to school then I ran to the barn and rode my mule away. I had never given him a name, only called him mule until now. "I think I'll call you Pegasus from now on, mule."

On Sunday the thirtieth, I got up an hour before dawn and watched the sun come up with Alex. I knew that he was watching the same sun from the place he waited to meet God. I wished that he would get out and run like the wind and never die. My mother and I dressed and walked slowly to the Baptist church. The sky had suddenly clouded over as if the heavens were preparing to cry at midnight. Church would be held inside instead of at the park.

The waxen-faced preacher opened the service. "Lord, we come to your house today to pray for Alex Campbell's soul." The church was packed to its limit and the doors were left open. The entrance under the bell spire was filled, and the flight of steps leading up was filled. The yard could hold no more.

She pushed her way through the crowd. She walked down the aisle toward the minister, her head held high and tears streaming down her face. Becky held her hand tightly and looked straight ahead also, neither left nor right. I knew she was coming but I don't know how I knew and suddenly I left my seat and reached Becky's hand and walked the aisle with them. When we reached the front of the church, she turned and squared her shoulders. Cayro Taylor told Chickasaw. She choked and coughed violently. The emotions she felt at this moment were overwhelming, something she wasn't prepared to contend with. She almost whispered, "Somebody's got to save him. I'm having his child."

My mother rushed down the aisle and grabbed my hand and pulled me to the door. We ran home, stopping only once for her to take her shoes off. She went directly to the phone and furiously turned the hand crank. "Get me the sheriff's office, Sister Ruby." She shouted into the mouth piece. "Stay on the line after you get him I need to call the governor and the warden at Reidsville." I got close to her so I could hear the sheriff's conversation.

After many precious minutes had passed, the sheriff came on the line. "Sheriff Gaines speaking."

"Cayro Taylor's having Alex's baby. Can we get a stay until they can get married?"

"I don't know. I'll call the judge. Hell, I'll go get him out of bed and sober him up."

She called General Pemberton and told him what had transpired. I could hear his loud voice. "I'm less than ten minutes from the governor's mansion. I'll be waiting for him when he gets home from church."

"Get me the state prison at Reidsville, Sister Ruby," she said when the General hung up.

Sister Ruby told her, "If they turn Alex out, he's going to drop dead with a heart attack knowing Cayro admitted that."

My mother was exasperated. "How on earth do you know everything that goes on in this town?"

Miss Ruby didn't hesitate. "I make it my business to find out, Clementine. How else would you suggest the news to be spread? We don't have a decent newspaper here. By the by, I wouldn't worry too much about calling Reidsville prison, your daddy, O. Z., and that wiff, Carlton, headed over there before church service was over. I suspect they will figure a way to stop the execution. Cayro's confession paused church, your running out stopped it, and those men leaving for Reidsville left Preacher Cauley talking to an empty church."

The warden wasn't in his office at the state prison, but the guard who answered the phone told my mother that he would go straight to the warden's house and make sure he knew that the sheriff or governor might call. "There's some of Mr. Campbell's friends in the courtyard. You want I should tell them anything?"

"Not yet." She depressed the phone cradle several times. "Sister Ruby, will you screen any calls coming to the house, and if it isn't someone important tell them that I can't tie up the line?" We heard a timid knock on the front door, and my mother walked through the hall, with me close behind, and opened the door. Mrs. Taylor and Becky were standing there. Their eyes were puffy and red. My mother opened her arms and the two women embraced and cried for a full five minutes.

When they finally calmed down, the four of us sat close to the phone and waited. My mother and Miss Cayro sat close, and occasionally one would reach over and squeeze the hand of the other. Someone else knocked, and I opened the door this time. Wash and Mrs. Jackson were there, and they came in and waited with us. I heard the back door slam, and in a second Lucy stuck her head in the door where we sat. "Me and Queen's going to be fixing supper for y'all. Go on talking and visiting, and don't mind us." Chilie came and stood in the door looking at the floor. He was wringing his hat between his big hands like a washrag, and his lower lip drooped sadly.

Pete said one time that when the end of the earth came, Chilie would be right there talking away, explaining everything. And the only thing that would shut the man up was for the angels to start blowing their trumpets for all saved souls to get in line. Man, I hoped the angels weren't coming.

We had an old French clock with the brass figurines of two dancing children on each side of the clock face. It was striking one when the telephone rang, and we all jumped. "Hello," my mother spoke into the bell-shaped mouthpiece. "Yes sir, Governor. I'm positive. She's sitting here now. Sir?" Her face fell and her voice started to tremble like a frightened kitten. "You can't mean this. At least let them have a wedding. Don't let a baby suffer your harshness." She paused and listened, and her tears were infectious. She replaced the phone on the cradle. A feeling of gloom settled around.

Bama Jo opened the door and walked in. Her smile froze, then turned from bewilderment to anger. "That no-good, scum-sucking pig of a son of a bitch." She sat next to my mother and her chin quivered until she lost control.

Sister Ruby did her job well. The few that called, came in wearing sadness like a shroud. Preacher Cauley walked in, and the sadness he felt mirrored the sadness here. He walked to my mother then Mrs. Taylor, hugging each. "The Lord will have the red carpet out for Alex. Don't either of you fret for his salvation. Even though he killed a man, God will welcome him."

I had felt numb since church, hearing and understanding some things, and understanding some things without hearing. I had listened to it all. Something was wrong and needed to be set right. "He didn't kill anyone," I told the group. No one seemed to pay any attention. After a measure of time Bama Jo looked at me and her eyes widened.

"Say that again, Luke."

"He didn't kill anybody. I heard him talking to God when we came home from Atlanta. He said he never killed anybody." Everyone in the room looked at me. I felt a heat rising in my body and I wanted to leave the room and run.

Bama Jo read my mind. "You sit right down. If you get up to run, I'll catch you. Now tell me what he said."

I told them as best as I could remember. "Call the sheriff," Bama Jo said to anyone who would respond. The preacher picked up the phone and handed it to Bama Jo. The sheriff picked up on the first ring. "Are you positive Alex killed Reuben?" Bama Jo shouted.

The sheriff answered loud. I could hear the sheriff say, "As positive as a man can be, who heard him say he did it."

"Did you have an autopsy done?"

"No ma'am. The county coroner turned in his report and I read it several times. He said Reuben died in his bed. Shot six times."

Bama Jo was grappling now, her thoughts outrunning the things she could ask the man. She asked if he would stay near his phone and hung up. She shared with the group the sheriff's part of the conversation.

Chilie wrung his hat and listened, as did the rest of us. A lapse of silence followed Bama Jo's recounting. I felt an unexplained tugging to watch Chilie. His eyes were wide and looking at the ceiling, or maybe through the ceiling, to something in his mind. "'Scuse me. Beg pardon."

Everyone looked at the big black man. "What is it, Chilie?" My mother asked.

"Some'ins not right. Mr. Luke's pistol was a Smith. Only shot five times. You said that man was shot six times."

"He might have reloaded," the preacher reasoned.

My mother looked at him. "No. I don't think so. Lucy said he ran to the hall closet and grabbed his pistol." Everyone was silent for a minute, and Bama Jo said excitedly, "Who's the coroner? Who the hell picked up the body?"

Chilie answered, "Mr. Linwood is both. He picked the body up and he's the county coroner."

Bama Jo snatched the phone. "Miss Ruby, get Mr. Linwood and you can listen in."

Fate was with us. Mr. Linwood was home taking a Sunday afternoon nap. She asked him about several things, then waited and made sure she remembered all she had to ask before she thanked him. He spoke softly so I didn't hear anything he said. She turned toward the pensive group, and the corners of her mouth gave her away before she spoke.

"He was shot six times with a forty-five-caliber bullet. Once in the arm, once in his knee, two in his abdomen, one through his heart, and one hit his little finger." She waited for the implications to sink in. "He was dressed in white under-shorts and nothing else. All but two of the bullets went through the bedcovers. Mr. Linwood said the first bullet probably killed Reuben. He said the bedcovers weren't disheveled. And he said, when I asked if Reuben was drunk, that when he embalms a body the odor of alcohol is almost overpowering. He said Reuben was not drunk." She waited a moment. "Alex lied. Someone else shot Reuben early that morning. Before he got out of bed." She tried to contain her excitement, tried to not verbalize her thoughts, but the obstruction that stayed her voice fled. Her eyes involuntarily looked toward the second floor. "I think Beth shot Reuben."

What happened after that was a blur. My mother went to talk to Beth. To see if she could penetrate the armor put in place to protect herself. Bama Jo clicked the phone until Sister Ruby finally screamed in her shrill voice for whoever was doing that please stop immediately. She got Sheriff Gaines on the phone.

"He didn't kill Reuben. Alex wouldn't shoot a man who was asleep." She detailed what Mr. Linwood had told her and what Chilie told her about Alex's pistol. The sheriff told her to hold on while he checked his evidence file and looked at the pistol Alex surrendered. She listened to the sheriff's loud voice, and I strained, in vain, to hear.

She told us, "He left to go to Judge Greer's house. He said he'd handle it from this point. It's less than nine hours until they execute Alex. I'm not going to risk letting a man handle a damned thing. If you want something done, get a woman to do it, I say." She and Miss Ruby settled down to the arduous task of tracking lawyers and appellate judges, congressmen, and any official other than the governor. He had made it clear that he wouldn't accept any more phone calls from our group.

I went to Beth's room to wait with my mother. She was telling Beth about everything that had happened. I think she was replaying all the events for her own benefit. She knew that Beth couldn't hear. My mother was simply talking, soothingly, to reach the wounded woman's spirit. My mother had focused her attention out the window as she spoke. I sat on the bed with Beth, who slowly reached and squeezed my hand. I saw her eyes were wet. I knew she would be back one day.

We spent the remainder of the day, some of us waiting, Bama Jo on the telephone. She wasn't getting what she wanted. Her temper flared occasionally and turned the air blue. Becky, Wash, and me fidgeted, groaned, played rock-paper-and-scissors, and watched the clock tick slower and slower. At six o'clock Bama Jo and Miss Ruby quit. Wasn't anybody else to call that would answer. The only thing to do was wait.

Bama Jo said to herself, I figured, to give reason to why Alex had done what he did. "I never knew anyone like him. Alex was willing to do whatever it took to keep Beth from going through what she would have been put through if they charged her with murder. I didn't know there was anyone that unselfish. She couldn't be charged with anything when she got back to normal, if he had already confessed and been executed."

We waited. My mother came down from Beth's room. Wash had curled up under the piano and gone to sleep. "Beth is going to be all right," was all she said.

A few minutes past eleven that night we heard a siren in the distance. Low at first, then getting louder. The sheriff's car pulled up in our yard about five seconds after the mayor had slid his tires around the corner, barely missing the mailbox and finally stopping at the front walk, dust flying everywhere. He hopped out grinning as the sheriff slid to a stop. "Whoop. By damn and hell. Whoop. We outrun you fair and square, Gaines. By God, I ought to be a race driver. If these folks hadn't of been so scared I'd of left you a hundred miles back." He looked in his car at his white-faced passengers. Alex, Pete, and Mr. O. Z. got out of the car. "Alex, old boy, have you got any drinking whiskey in your house? I know I promised Bama Jo I'd quit drinking, and I am just as soon as I get through celebrating. Come on in, Gaines, and have a drink with me."

The sheriff was grinning too. "I might have one or two with you, Carlton."

Alex stopped the sheriff. "I need to speak to you in private." Because of me being small they didn't notice I stayed.

Everyone left. I suspect the liquor was more important than the conversation. Alex said, "He pardoned me. Does this mean that no one else can be charged with the crime?"

"The state charged you, and the governor pardoned you. You confessed to the crime, but we all know Beth did it."

"Does this mean no one else can be charged?" Louder.

"The way I interpret the law, nobody can be charged. You confessed and were pardoned."

"Gaines, I killed the son of a bitch. If she wakes up and says anything different, I killed him."

"Alex, whatever happened, I don't want to know. It's over."

The two of them walked into the house. I followed, not understanding. Cayro Taylor stood there white-faced with tears streaking her face. "Alex, I'm sorry."

He didn't know what to do, so he hugged her then walked briskly up the stairs to Beth. When he came down, the women had supper ready in only that effortless way women get these things done. The men had made several trips out to Pete's car, and each time they came in I think they were trying to see who could talk loudest. Alex couldn't keep his eyes off Cayro. I was going to have an uncle or aunt younger than I was. Godamighty.

Pete kept grinning and slapping Alex on the back. "I guess we'd best go shopping for a new suit come tomorrow, eh, Alex? Looks like we've got a right imminent wedding coming up. Anyone else want to go suit shopping? I'm paying at Lonnie's."

Mr. O. Z. spoke up, "Pete we've got a good half-case of Canadian left down at the station."

"Well, taking into consideration what we'll be celebrating. I'm not going to object to your idea, O. Z." The wide grin never left his face.

Mrs. Jackson pushed her untouched plate away and said loudly, "Pete, I know you're going to be mad with me, but I don't care. And you can wipe that grin off your face too.

I went with Cayro to Doctor Ellis when she found out she was expecting, and I had an examination too. I know how tight-fisted you two are, and a double wedding would be cheaper, so that's what I'm suggesting."

My God, were Sister Ruby and Miss Grace going to stay up late tomorrow.

Epilogue

I N LATE WINTER, Beth smiled at me one day. The next day I took her a fistful of daffodils. She reached out for them, and the bright yellow reflected in her large eyes, moving now. She spoke in a strange, low voice, "Ah, the daffodil, that shows its head before the swallows dare, and make the winds sweet."

Alex spent hours each day trying to rekindle her interest in living. Mrs. Taylor was now my step-grandmother, as was Mrs. Jackson. I didn't have enough sense to figure out what kin Becky and Wash were to me now.

One morning in the spring Alex walked down the stairs from Beth's room and sat down on the bottom tread, rubbing his arm and chest. Doctor Ellis came and called Mr. Linwood to take Alex to the hospital in Trinity after he told us Alex had had a heart attack.

I watched the bluebirds that spring as they built their nests in the abandoned holes the woodpecker had used and left. There weren't nearly as many this year.

Me and Pete go down to Alex's grave at least twice a week. Sometimes he just stands there. Those days he won't talk to me at all.